THE COLLECTORS

GREG JOLLEY

THE COLLECTORS

A NOVEL

Livonia, Michigan

Edited by Amanda Lewis and Hannah Ryder

THE COLLECTORS

Published by BHC Press

Library of Congress Control Number: 2020936635

ISBN: 978-1-64397-177-3 (Hardcover)
ISBN: 978-1-64397-178-0 (Softcover)
ISBN: 978-1-64397-179-7 (Ebook)

For information, write:
BHC Press
885 Penniman #5505
Plymouth, MI 48170

Visit the publisher:
www.bhcpress.com

Dedicated to
Ryan Hill

Thank you

Walter Potter's Curious World of Taxidermy

Alexander Jansson, the artist, for the
magical constructions and scenes

Benjamin Lacombe, the artist—for the expressions, for the eyes

The Gold Rush film production team

Cinematography Theory and Practice by Blair Brown

The wide music of "When You Come Back Down" by Nickel Creek

All my dear friends at The Well

Lauren Humphries-Brooks, editor extraordinaire

Amanda Lewis for a brilliant final

In memory of
Rosalia Lombardo
Jayne Mansfield
James Dean

THE COLLECTORS

CHAPTER ONE

◆ ◆ ◆

TIN CAN

"WELCOME TO the film set, Mr. Kiharazaka. Please mind your step, we're having a problem with vermin."

The tall, thin man, fresh from Kyoto, adjusted his stride, placing each step of his spacesuit boots gingerly.

"I'm Rolf. Can I call you Zaka?" the assistant director went on.

"Please, no," Mr. Kiharazaka replied demurely.

"Got it."

"Will we be going weightless? It was in the original scene."

"We're woking on that, yes."

"Woking?"

"A joke. Sort of."

A few yards away, green gaffing tape marked the edge of the darkened film set. Rolf spoke into her headset and the lights came up, revealing the interior of the spacecraft: the complex helm and seating for the crew. The second set—the crew table and galley kitchen—was half-lit in the distance.

Mr. Kiharazaka stared with unreserved delight. The crew had accurately replicated the 1990s television series *Tin Can*'s two most famous locations.

Members of the film crew were already on the set, at their places among the equipment; lights, extended boom mics, and various cameras, some dollied and some shoulder-held. Mr. Kiharazaka had to rotate stiffly in his spacesuit, turning his helmet, visor up, to watch the young, professional film crew. He nodded to some and spoke to none. For the most part, these serious professionals looked right through him, focused on their craft.

"Please step in, Zaka. We'd like you to feel comfortable in both locations."

"Where is the cast? The Robbins family?"

"Soon enough. Please." Rolf extended her hand and Zaka crossed the green tape and stepped into the helm, noting that the flooring was white painted plywood. With the flight helmet on, the voices about the set were muted. Zaka stared at the helm, admiring, but not touching, the multiple displays. He stood back of Captain Robbins's helm chair, taking in all the exacting details of the complex spacecraft controls. Easing between the captain and copilot chair, he turned to Rolf with his white gloved hand out to the second chair and asked, "May I?"

Rolf gave him her buttery professional smile.

"Captain, permission to man the helm?" Zaka asked.

Rolf rolled her eyes, up into the complex scaffolding above. The client was already in role, using the famous and familiar dialogue from the *Tin Can* series. Since none of the cast was yet on set, Rolf answered for Matt Stuck, the sod of an actor who played Captain Robbins.

"Aye, mate. Take *thar* helm," She spoke the next well-known line with a grimace.

Zaka bowed to her voice and twisted around into the copilot's chair.

She looked on as Zaka began the familiar series of taps and changes on the right side of the helm. She could hear him identifying each click and adjustment he made. He was doing a good job mimicking the terse, focused voice of copilot Sean Robbins, but his inflections were clearly Japanese.

The director, Rose Daiss, entered the soundstage, crossed to the set, and for once didn't trip on the snakes of cables. She wobbled her large rear into the La-Z-Boy with "Director" stenciled on the back. Her nickname was "Bottles" and never used in her presence—it was a reference to the many times she had washed up. Her pudgy face was nip-and-tuck stretched, her skin was rough, but rouged well. She did have good hair.

The director's personal assistants entered the soundstage and roamed to their places just back of the cameras. They donned headsets and leisurely took up their positions, standing deferentially to Bottles's side, their faces lit by the glow of their tablets.

Rolf shouted for status among the film's crews, and they called back equally loud. Lighting, boom mics, and cameras leaned in on the set. Mr. Zaka climbed from the helm and walked back into the spacecraft along the equipment bays on the left wall—the right wall of equipment didn't exist, providing the view for one of the many cameras. He tapped a brief series on the wall panel and the air lock door opened with a gasp. He stepped through, the door closing at his heels, and crossed the short area of soundstage to the side entrance of the crew and kitchen set. Zaka took in every detail of the reproduced *Tin Can* galley as he moved carefully through the room. He eased himself into his role and the chair assigned to Ruth Robbins, the flight crew's matriarch.

The director shouted at her assistants, barking orders and questions, sounding semi-lucid. Rose's drug-addled, fast-clipped voice received intimidated replies. She was enjoying their pale, cowering expressions while chasing two lines of thought, a mixture of movie-making aesthetics and redundant direction. Her face was beading with drug sweat on her upper lip and brow.

"*Where's my cast?*" Rose bellowed, finishing the tirade. That done, she promptly nodded off, delighting Rolf, who then inherited the director's role.

Zaka was exploring the many displays embedded in the galley table, trying to ignore the shouting.

"Heat it up," Rolf instructed her underling.

The assistant typed a series of brief commands on his tablet and the script dialogue for Ruth Robbins—whom Zaka had paid dearly to portray—appeared. The script was scroll ready and at an angle on the galley table that couldn't be seen by the cameras.

Rolf heard the cast crossing to the set, a scuffing of moon boots and voices approaching from the soundstage. A sweeping flashlight beam guided their way. The cast moved into the back glow from the lights on the set. Rolf pressed the inside of her cheek between her teeth and bit down. Most of the original cast had been hired or *persuaded* to appear in the remake of the famous season seven-ending catfight scene. The brawl between the Robbins' daughters was nominally, impotently, refereed by the only member of the flight crew who was not a member of the family: the handsome, irreverent, and sociopathic engineer, Greer Nails.

Twenty-two years had been most unkind to the once-famous family members. Greer Nails appeared overinflated; his penchant for food and wine and dessert over the past years of dimming celebrity had taken its toll. His formerly idolized face was jowled, reddened, and fat. His spacesuit looked like a white dirigible.

The other cast members were naked save their space helmets. Time and gravity and overindulgence had also taken a toll on their bodies. Greer Nails was the lone holdout from nudity, and with obese good reason.

The scene that Zaka had chosen from the menu provided by the studio had cost him a breathless $3.7 million. An additional $1.3 million was invoiced when he selected the option off the premiere menu for the cast to be nude except for space helmets. He had expressed his desire to be part of the famous scene's reenactment, in the role of Ruth Robbins, the space family matriarch. Most of his role was to be aghast at the start of a violent family shouting match and brawl. Later, he would be able to view the vignette time and again, for all eternity, receiving sole ownership of the footage of this and the other short scene as part of the package he had paid for.

Zaka watched his castmates approach, trying to keep his eyes on their helmets, not their nakedness. He was delighted and light headed with his proximity to the famous—the real flesh instead of celluloid, but their memorized faces were distorted by their helmets.

Nods were used in lieu of greetings. They had met during rehearsal earlier in the day. Places were taken, and Rolf reviewed the lighting and camera placements.

The first scene was succinctly re-rehearsed. This was of little use to Zaka, who had the script committed to memory. But the rehearsal helped him dissolve some of his lighter-than-air headiness. The rest of the cast drolly joined the read- and walk-through, their acting marked by a blend of boredom, professionalism, and chemicals.

Zaka was delighted. Here he was, a real actor with an important part in the infamous scene's reenactment. It was all he could do to not giggle. He somehow found the ability to maintain Ruth Robbins's dithering mothering role.

Julianne, the slutty, smart sister, stepped past Greer and pantomimed the jerk-off gesture that would set off her sibling, "Cy," as in Cyborg. In the television series, Cy had been Greer Nail's budding romantic interest.

Zaka was enthralled, but also concerned. He had paid for Captain Robbins to sit at the head of the galley table, and he was nowhere to be seen.‑A booming, authoritative voice carried from the back of the soundstage.

"Welcome to *Tin Can Two*, Mr. Kiharazaka. You are certainly star material, mm-hmm!" Fatima Mosley called out.

Fatima was the studio head, noticeably short and burdened by a massive chest that gave her stride a wobble. She was dressed in an elegant and trendy style, including a beret. She had a titanium leg, the original lost to disease. The metal ratcheted when her knee articulated.

"Zaka's doing a great job," Rolf called over, not turning from the rehearsal.

"It's Kiharazaka, please," Zaka politely corrected Rolf again.

"Actually, it's Ruth Robbins." Fatima smiled, causing her cheeks to fill and her eyes to disappear.

Zaka flushed with pride at being addressed as Ruth.

"All is well, mm-hmm?" Fatima asked Zaka.

"Yes, yes. Might I ask? Is Captain Robbins ready? And son Sean Robbins?"

"Why, here's Sean now," Fatima answered, her crunched face dissolving downward, revealing her wise, ferret eyes. She didn't explain Captain Robbins's absence, and Zaka showed good manners by not repeating his question.

Sure enough, Sean Robbins, the *Tin Can*'s copilot, appeared from the shadows of the soundstage, naked save his helmet and boots, looking slightly sedated—well, a lot sedated. His birdlike wrists hung limp.

There was a white worm of drool creeping from his face, now ravaged by years of amphetamine addiction. He was escorted by two of the bigger grips, who held his scarecrow-thin arms and pulled him along, his moon boots sketching the soundstage flooring.

The sisters, Cy and Julianne, did not look pleased to be reanimating their once-famous daughter roles, no matter the money. They were clearly drugged to an agitated condition and firing foul slurs, even before the shoot began. Julianne had a wrench tattoo on her naked, once-perfect boob. Cy's sensual body was scarecrow thin, as though drawn of all blood.

The grips assisted Sean Robbins into the hot lights and seated him at the galley table. He opened one eye and panned it across the cameras and lights aimed on him, then barfed into his own lap.

"Unpleasant, mm-hmm," Fatima observed.

Zaka did the brave thing—he stayed in role, putting on his best Mrs. Robbins bemused and maternal expression.

"Nice," Rolf encouraged him.

One of the grips wiped up Sean's vomit. The other cleaned off his chest. Sean stood up and looked on, patting one of the men on the top of the head.

Rolf called out, "I have the set!"

From the film crews came sharp, short calls, and the boom mics lowered overhead.

"Quiet, quiet!" Rolf delighted in her temporary directing role.

"Lock it up," she hollered.

"Places," she shouted to the cast.

"Cameras up!"

"Roll sound."

"Roll camera."

A young woman appeared with an electric slate, shouted a brief stream of incomprehensible code, clacked the device, and disappeared.

Zaka did well, not looking to Captain Robbins's empty seat at the head of the table.

Rolf yelled, "Action," and the movie magic began.

For Zaka, there was a spiritual lift, even as he stayed in his rehearsed movements. He allowed himself to experience the elation, but stayed in the role of motherly concern.

Julianne entered the scene from the door to the helm. She moved behind Sean, who had a line of dialogue but missed. Staring at Cy, she stepped to Greer's side and hefted the weight of his groin. Cy transitioned fast and smooth, from agog to madness. She fired forward and attacked, going for the smirk on her sister's face with a clawed left hand and the space cup in the other.

As scripted, Mrs. Robbins took one step back from her end of the table, her expression alarmed and offended.

Greer was looking down at his groped crotch like he was just then realizing he had one. He leaned back as Cy collided with Julianne, and the brawl exploded with screams and nails and fists. The two careened off the galley counter and shelving, swinging and connecting blows.

If Captain Robbins had been at the head of the table, he would have moved fast to separate the two, looking sad and determined and disappointed. Instead, a bit of ad lib occurred, the two brawlers tumbling low in the shot, fists and knees swinging and pumping. Greer performed the ad lib, turning to the mayhem with a slack expression and barfing on himself again.

Mrs. Robbins went into action. She stomped manfully to her scuffling daughters, arms *shooing*, intending to break up the chaos on the spaceship floor. She was two strides away when Greer stepped out and pushed her back. Mrs. Robbins resisted, flailing her arms, eyes wide with alarm. Greer held her true. The fight continued, the sisters grunting and gasping. Hair was grabbed, a low fist was thrown. Julianne coughed in pain. Cy let out a cry, "You bitch!"

That was Zaka's cue. He looked away, eyes upward and spoke the season-ending line, "My daughters. The sluts."

"Cut. Cut. Cuu. Cuush..." Rose Daiss, the replaced director, called out in a trailing off slur. She was ignored.

The brawl continued. A mangy rat crossed the plywood set boards, scurrying away from the fisticuffs. The two beefy grips stepped to the edge of the set, poised to separate the sisters. The brawl looked real enough to them.

Rolf took the director's prerogative, screaming at everyone.

"Cut!"

◆ ◆ ◆

THE SECOND and final shot of the day was set in the spaceship helm. It was to be filmed out of sequence, being the preceding scene to the one just completed. The naked cast and Zaka stepped into the second set after the crew rolled it into position, replacing the galley. It was more efficient to move these than the cameras, lights, and crews. The grips roughly encouraged Sean Robbins to stand and take his copilot seat at the helm.

Zaka as Ruth Robbins took up his position at the back of her husband's seat, her hands on the sides, her eyes studying his expert and forceful control of the ship. It was a struggle because the seat was vacant. On the complex display, an alarm blinked and rang.

The entire movie set rattled briefly underneath his space boots. Zaka looked directly to the cameras—a big *no-no*, as he had been instructed. The soundstage tilted and then straightened.

"It's a special effect," Rolf called to Zaka, more so than the rest of the cast. The daughters appeared startled as they grabbed at the padded helm walls for support. The set leaned back and leveled. No one commented. Zaka did a commendable job of returning to his role as the matriarch.

Rehearsal began. Off set, the young film crew were talking in clipped, soft voices to one another and into their headsets.

Fatima thumbed her cell phone on and walked away into the black shadows of the soundstage. She and Rolf spoke briefly before she left the soundstage, her metal knee clacking softer and softer as she disappeared from the set.

In the steel-walled first hallway, she put her beefy hand on the wall for balance and kicked at a passing rat with her good leg. The animal screeched as it careened off the wall, its back legs peddling, its lower back broken. Fatima extinguished it with her heel to its head and walked on. The narrow hall made a series of tight turns, under offensive fluorescent lightbulbs caged in metal. The ceiling was low and lined with pipes, of no matter to the very short Fatima. She arrived at the last steel door at the end of the last hall.

Inside was a richly decorated small film set that featured the long and deep casting couch as well as a padded gymnast bench and a four-post bed, this last with adjustable stirrups. The room was decorated to resemble what the premiere package offered as the optional "Ye Olde Casting Couch." The cameras, lights, and sound equipment were behind the faux sixteenth-century, five-by-five mirror on the east wall. Zaka had not chosen this from the menu.

"What a shame," Fatima grumbled as she opened the next door. The Ye Olde was an easy moneymaker.

The last room had a raised, rounded metal door with a spinning, centered handle. Fatima struggled briefly getting the first turn on the wheel to happen before it spun easily.

Her eyes went directly to Captain Robbins, who was laying down but far from relaxed. He did not look at all happy. In fact, he appeared terrorized and panicked. His nude, flabby body was fish-belly white in the stage arc lighting. He only wore the white plastic helmet, the visor raised.

"How's it going?" Fatima asked him sweetly. It was a rhetorical question—she had tired of his entreaties, his pleas, his new willingness to play his part in the reenacted *Tin Can*.

The captain made a series of *arf* sounds, and his rotund body twisted and shook.

"About the nudity—that was your issue, not mine," she told him, stepping into the glare of the studio lighting. "You knew the filming was for a private collector. Not for general release to the public. That would be a real ratings challenge."

She smiled and her cheeks hid her eyes and he screamed.

"Stuffy in here," she said and worked a lever beside the wood gurney he was strapped to. The room's single window opened with the sound of metal sliding against metal. Fresh salted air breezed into the room.

She pulled a second lever, and the row of rollers underneath the captain began to rotate. He turned his wild pleading eyes from Fatima to his extended, pudgy feet. Between his toes and the open window was the mouth of a chum machine, a Make-A-Bait Model 27.

Inside the mouth were spinning rows of metal blades.

Fatima noted the light on the control panel change from green to red, indicating that the film crew behind the large mirror was in place. Fatima patted the captain's shoulder before removing his plastic space helmet. He was all wide eyes on her, a terrified expression, and sweat-tangled hair.

"We're an environment-friendly studio," she said to the captain. Setting the helmet aside, she pulled a third lever, and the teeth on the Make-A-Bait began to spin at high speed. "We recycle."

The green light began to blink, indicating three seconds to the start of filming. Fatima nodded her round head, smiling, showing approval of the captain's immense screams. He was finding words, "No!" and "Please!" among groans and tears.

She let him carry on like that for three minutes, until his voice was nothing but hoarse rasping between heavy panting.

Fatima donned a plastic apron and leaned close to the captain's reddened face and jerking eyes.

"Now, now," she cooed. "You made your choice not to be in *Tin Can*. Your choice got us to this situation. This *other* final scene. Already have two bids for the footage."

She pulled the finger throttle on the second lever and the gears for the rollers under the gurney engaged.

The captain's feet and shins entered the Make-A-Bait and exited in a red-and-purple spray. As expected, some back spray splattered Fatima's apron.

"Puree? Oh, no, this won't do, mm-hmm." She adjusted the machine to Bait Chunks.

He was screaming. She yelled into the madness in a calm voice. "Think of this as your final scene. And guess what? You're the star!"

Bite-sized chunks were blowing out through the window. The spinning metal teeth were into Captain Robbins's knees.

"Wow, you're not bad! For once, little ham at all."

CHAPTER TWO

◆ ◆ ◆

WILLY

I WAS standing on the roof of a 1948 Packard Model 2293 Station Sedan, gazing out over a sea of faded but not rusted Packards, circa 1946–1956. This area of the warehouse was nicely segregated by year, but still chaotic. Seventy-thousand square feet of parts, rebuilds, and partial restorations.

In my hands, I had the front seat covers that reversed from cloth to leather. These were a new feature of the 1956 Packard Caribbean convertible. All I had to find in this graveyard of metal was a 1948 Model 2293 dash-mounted rearview mirror. The Model 2293 I was on the roof of had already been cannibalized. I jumped one roof over, mumbling, "Hmm, *rearview* mirror? Is there any other kind?"

Times were good. Gustin's Packard Restorations could absorb Howie's appetite for losses and wasting money. Gustin's could flame out just like Packard did in 1956; both not big enough to not fail. The company had a backlog of orders, so we worked the most lucrative rebuilds first. Gustin's had twelve employees, not including Howie Gustin, the owner, who handled sales from the tables of the finer Detroit restaurants, the ones that brought a telephone to his table.

When Packard was shuttered in '56, he sold seven-hundred acres of fine walnut groves and went on a Packard shopping spree—a sure sign at the time that Howie was a wee bit nuts. He didn't buy Packards; he bought stocks of postwar Packard parts.

My compadre, Dot, was good with the transmission and suspension, even the complex Ultramatic automatic transmissions. I preferred to work on gathering the lighter-to-carry decorative parts, leaving him to lay on his rolling cart underneath hundreds of pounds of steel. There's not a speck of aluminum or plastic anywhere on a Packard. Dot's brilliance was the under-the-hood work. If I told you his first name or if he ever shaved off the beard and got a haircut, you'd remember him, recognize him. He was once famous. Now he's content. Serene.

And there he was. My best friend had gone wide these past years; not fat, just strong and outward. He was easing between two 1947 Clipper four-doors with his cellphone to his ear, which he wasn't talking to, but pointing at. His eyes were on me. I watched him disappear behind an elevated Caribbean. When I saw him again, he was at the edge of the row of 1946–1956s, where I still stood on the roof of a 1949 four-door.

He removed his dark welding goggles, and there were his beautiful expressive eyes. I can always see the Dot of old, the movie idol who swept women's hearts and then men admired. He held up the phone while those amazing gray-blue eyes above a sideways smile steadied on me.

"Your cell? Been calling you," he said, standing at the shiny, ornate grill and bumper of the Station Sedan.

"Lost it," I replied.

"Again?"

"Well…"

"Intentionally?"

I knew that one was rhetorical. Dot climbed the bumper and onto the domed hood, stepping respectfully over the chrome ornament—that swan with raised wings and sad, lowered head. He walked up along the hood to me. I sat down on the roof with my boots also on the hood, which was large enough for us to dance on if we chose.

I was smiling. Until he reached inside his coveralls and took out a telegram.

"Oh," was the best I could come up with.

"Yeah," Dot said, handing it to me.

I know exactly three people who actually use that archaic form of communication. My sons still do so when writing to their mom, indulging her delight and preference for telegrams, an archaic service with few remaining providers. The boys didn't use them to contact me. They preferred phone calls, so I knew who this one was from; my wife, soon-to-be ex, the wondrous Pauline Place. Yes, *her*. The famous actress and, like Dot, also the spark for movie-audience wonder, inspiring women to fawn and men to breathe badly.

I unfolded the sheet and read the dot-matric print in all caps. I read it twice.

PIE YOU AND I ARE IN A CYCLONE BUT
I AM IN SERIOUS TROUBLE -(STOP)-
I NEED A RESCUE I KNOW OH THE DRAMA
-(STOP)- RHONDA CAN GET YOU TO ME -(STOP)-
PLEASE COME -(STOP)-

Dot stood patiently, not saying a word, waiting for me to remark, which I did with my usual verbosity. "Oh."

I slid down the right side of the two-piece windshield, resting my rear on the long-curved plane of the Packard's hood. Dot stepped back, giving me some space. I watched him study my eyes and expression. Bet I was looking deflated, at best.

"Gonna be traveling?" he asked.

"Looks so. For a while."

"Want a ride to the airport?"

"Please."

"Didja find all of the '48 rearview?" he asked. He knew the game well. The original mirror mounting screws were as important as the mirror itself. The wealthy Packard collectors insisted on this level of detail.

"No, but I will."

"Wanna go to the airport during lunch break?"

"That works. Gives me time to find the mirror."

"Don't forget the screws."

◆ ◆ ◆

I CLIMBED into Dot's car still wearing my stained and grimy coveralls instead of street clothes. He looked me over and didn't comment. Putting his '53 Buick Roadmaster in gear, we were soon out among modern-day cars. And modern-day pace. Dot navigated the big old Buick with smooth hands and feet on the peddles, keeping us to the slow lanes, not because of lack of pace, but lack of stress and scurry. And traveling in style. We cruised south on Highway 23 and swung onto Highway 94 for the Detroit airport.

"First sign of Christmas," Dot said. We had been riding along in comfortable silence.

I looked out into the swarm of automobiles around us. That's all I saw.

"The migration of pine trees bound on rooftops." Dot explained.

Why, of course.

We bypassed the queues of cars and taxis and buses, each disgorging happy holiday travelers and stern-faced business men and women. Past the many airline marques, Dot steered into the narrow lane to the private terminals a quarter mile away from the bustling main terminal. Although it'd been a couple of years since either of us had taken a flight, Dot navigated us straight to the smallish Jet Thru parking area, pulling the huge Roadmaster to the curb with grace and ease. The brass and glass doors of the foyer slid open before I had pulled on the hefty car door handle.

A lovely, sharply dressed young woman approached the car, standing beside my door.

"Baggage, Mr. Danser?" she asked.

"Always," Dot answered for me, leaning to the passenger-side window. I turned to her with him chuckling behind me; that once-famous coarse rumble of bemusement.

"He's mistaken," I told the young woman.

"See yah, Dot," I said, handing him the 1948 Model 2293 dash-mounted rearview mirror *and* mounting screws.

"I hope the trip is good and interesting," Dot replied with his oft repeated version of *so long*.

I followed the beautiful attendant inside, iced wind shoving at both of us. The heat inside was glorious, as was the décor of Jet Thru's lounge. An elegant seating area and dining room and bar with a media room off to the left. She asked for my safe key and disappeared. Except for a waiter and bartender at their stations, I was the only one there. I ignored the bar on ex-drunk instinct, considered the dining room and passed, making my way to a comfy, burnt-sienna leather couch facing the wall of windows. I considered my grimy coveralls a moment before sitting down, reclining back, and extending my work boots out on the deep carpeting. I looked back into the room one time, to the bartender, who gave me both a nod and a smile. He looked somewhat familiar—from long-ago days. Seemed he remembered me. I turned to the waiter, who appeared expectant and saddened. In these kinds of places, you never hear doors open or close. Nor the sound of footsteps. The place was classy enough to *not* have soft mood music spilling from the ceiling. People just magically appeared beside you and you sensed them nudging their aura, their bubble, against yours.

So it was with the teen, who wasn't really a teen, but younger than thirty and so deserving that. This one was dressed in a roughed-up beige: suit, shirt, even his boots. He had shoulder-length *beige* hair, a gaunt face, and wore pince-nez that gave his eyes a bug's serious focus.

And he was watching me, looking as expectant, as hopeful, as the bartender.

"Mr. Danser?" he said, sounding deferential and looking pleased.

I studied his clean-shaven face and rubbed my chin at the same time.

"Interesting," I said, ignoring his greeting. "These days, everyone over the age of nine has a beard."

"Can I join you?" he asked.

I was sitting to the left of the twelve-foot couch. I gestured to the free nine feet and decided to be polite instead of enjoying my solitude.

"Please," I offered.

Having been polite quite long enough, I turned my thoughts to the 1956 Packard Caribbean convertible. It would be a good runner, even if absurdly old. Damned thing was built before I was birthed. I'm an adoptee, and no, I'm not the least bit curious about mum and dud. Except I hope they loved. Had a romance. A future planned. Hopes and happiness and dreams. For their likely four minutes of bliss. For *all* four minutes. Enough on that.

The 1956 Packard Caribbean convertible was a healthy distraction from what I *could* be considering—where I was going and why: to my soon-to-be ex, the faultless, beautiful Pauline Place.

I realized that the teen was talking to me. I blinked and changed my focus. Even dug up my manners.

"I'm sorry. What?"

"You've ignored all my calls."

"Of course. I don't know you."

"I'm Ethan," and he included his last name, which rightfully floated away. Hearing *Ethan* was enough to put a label on his bubble.

"You're the writer."

"Well, no, sir. A researcher. Of your wife."

He opened his beige, shouldered haversack and searched for something.

I was pleased that he hadn't used her name so far in this slightly cozy chat. He had no place to do so with me and, truly, I didn't much care to hear it. I turned my eyes to him, allowing him about half of my attention and staying polite, no matter how tedious this was certainly going to be.

"What's your *angle*?" I asked, with only a slight edge. No, no, really.

"Her craft. This is my first chance to talk with you. I'm hoping you can—"

"Did you follow me here?"

"Yes. Of course."

I had to smile at him. I *do* admire brash.

"Your slant? What is it? Another bio? A *fanzine*?"

He absorbed that last without ire, and I liked that as well.

"I'm not the writer. I'm the collector. The researcher."

"Oh? Who's the author of this claptrap? Who reads those? Do you really think actors have anything to say?"

"It's not going to be another bio. The book will be about her acting craft."

"Oh. Good. She would appreciate that," I said sincerely. That tasted strange and rare.

"Yes, her life and career have been both microscoped enough—"

"You used microscope as a verb? I like that."

He blinked through a cloud of confusion.

"I misplaced my telephone." That was as close to an explanation he was getting about the ignored calls.

A platter of fine crystal glasses and silver bowl full of chipped ice lowered to the table before us. A green bottle of Tanqueray stood sentry beside the sliced limes. I looked at the bartender and it was clear he did remember me—the prior me. My old fondness for that deadly clear liquid and cruel, perfectly shaved ice.

"Compliments and enjoy," the bartender said.

"Wanna bet?" I turned away from the two crystal glasses that looked eager for ice and a splash of my past insanity.

"Sir?" he asked Ethan.

"Heavens no, thank you."

"Smart," I said.

The bartender walked away, leaving temptation on the low table.

"Do you know you resemble the Jan Michael Vincent?" he told me.

"I'm sorry, who? No, wait, an actor, right?"

"Yes, he was in—"

"Actors. Let me help you out. Most are chattel. Breathing furniture."

His steady eyes widened. I liked that too. His pince-nez bobbed. He changed tack.

"Headed to the missus?"

I looked at the tray of death at our knees. One of the crystal glasses had disappeared. My new acquaintance was casually closing his haversack.

I had to grin. "Did you nick a glass? No, don't answer."

I looked for an expression of guilt or faux innocence. It wasn't there.

I grinned some more.

"I collect," is all he said.

"Oh," I said with a splash of wry.

Another presence stepped to the couch.

"Mr. Danser, you're free to board," the young attendant said.

I looked to my couch-mate. Jeez, a clean-shaven puppy with insect eyes.

"Where're we going?" he asked.

"*We?*"

"I was hoping to bum a ride."

"Got your passport?"

"Will I need it?"

"Don't know."

"I have it."

We boarded the aircraft, a rather smallish, sleek jet. The interior was antiseptically modern and irritating: *my* money days were over, but not those of my soon-to-be ex-wife. Eggshell leather recliners and couches, teakwood for the trimmings, and that wonderfully appealing closed door beyond the salon.

Pausing at the open cockpit door, I nodded greetings to the pilot and copilot and ignored their kind replies. The dense array of electronics and control had my eyes. Far gone were the days I had learned to fly a much simpler aircraft with what looked like one-tenth of this jet's instruments. My limited flying time had been in treetop small prop planes, and I had never been licensed, but taught out of necessity for late-night cargo deliveries. That said, I worried. Do these two ever have a chance or need to look out the windshield?

"Mr. Danser, welcome aboard," was spoken in professional, sweet voice.

Cindy—I do read name tags—offered a charming smile with a dash of sass. A darling, adorable face and, oh my, a blend of amazing, complex scents from her throat and luxuriously coifed hair.

Ethan melted into a rear-facing recliner and I stretched my boots out from the middle of the couch. Cindy brought my satchel and set it beside me. She also handed me my passport from the airline safe.

Unlike the Jet Thru bartender, Cindy the stewardess had her client card memorized. She brought me a glass of chipped ice and a bottle of Fanta Grape.

She brought Ethan his requested glass of ice water, and the two of us sipped our drinks as the jet taxied and took off. When the plane leveled off at cruising altitude, I carried my satchel to that closed door at the back of the salon.

There was a pair of pajamas folded on the bed. I set my satchel beside them and undressed and entered the shower. As the warm water rinsed my head and shoulders, I slid down the tiles and sat. It was good to have some private time. Seems it had been days since I had been rummaging for car Packard parts, with the biggest concern being where Dot and I would go to dinner. Now I was headed to Pauline, a significant change in direction.

◆ ◆ ◆

OUR LOVE, our fine marriage is—*was*—always a dance. Often a deliriously surprising salsa of passion and laughter. Sometimes a ballroom waltz, other times all jazzy and flapping, sometimes all twist and shout, sometimes throwing plates and ashtrays, but at the walls, never at each other.

We also shared similar intellects. Endlessly curious, amused, and confident—no, we're both sure and cocky. We were parted often. In those days I was a respected cinematographer and Pauline was off to here and there around the planet for lengthy shoots. She's creative and, more to the point, hardworking, and a natural at her art and craft. But more than gifted with talent, she was relentless in her efforts to improve her understandings and abilities, exploring the complicated expressions and gestures of motivation and compulsions and confusions and all the black matter of evil—whatever her current role demanded.

The rub? We had been living in our separate orbits too long. On the phone and in her preferred use of telegrams, the laughter and wit had gotten dusty.

I got up and left the shower running and searched the vanity for a pair of scissors, then sat back down in the warm water. There were complimentary toiletries in a teak basket, and I shaved and scrubbed with bathing gel. I used the scissors to cut my own hair from my shoulders to collar height and clipped my bangs and sides. I expected a few laughs from my handiwork, but it was an improvement. I hoped.

For grins, I opened my old satchel—I'd last carried it when I made the rather large career change. Inside were three pairs of different-lensed eyeglasses and my director's lens on a strap. There were two pair of binoculars and a handheld viewfinder I had modified to carry around to take in the world, caring not at all for the odd stares of others. Closing the satchel, I considered being sociable and having dinner with the Ethan *teen*. Instead, I pulled on the pajamas and went to bed.

I was awakened by Cindy—lovely, scented Cindy—cooing and tapping on the door. My clothes had mysteriously been laundered and waited for me on the chair beside the bed.

Ethan was enjoying a two-course meal in the salon. He was working his large cellphone on the white linen table. Tapping and talking—it's what everyone did those days.

I sat down across from him.

Seemed someone had nicked my sterling silverware.

I grinned and asked for a grilled cheese sandwich.

"Tell me about your life as a cinematographer?" he swallowed and asked.

"Cameraman, please."

"If you prefer. You were once quite well known and respected."

I looked at his Moleskine notebook. He had a pen in his free hand.

"You gonna write this down?"

"Well, sure I—"

"Well, nothing. Don't and we can talk."

He asked me about the more successful films I had worked on, sometimes as a director of photography and other times as lead camera. Thankfully, he had questions about the craft rather than the *art*. He got me yakking a little. I admit I was soon well inflated. I turned the conversation away from that to my passion, former passion, for the Steadicam.

His large phone began to sing, light up, and vibrate. All at once. He tapped on it, and the sound and light show ended. He raised it to his ear and listened for a minute.

I watched his expression change from relaxed to vicious.

"Tie her up in legalese and frighten her witless. *Persuade* her."

Sounded like typical business chatter. It brought to mind my studio days. I chewed grilled cheese. Cindy poured me another Fanta over hand-shaved ice. I watched her do so and asked her if she would marry me.

Her first laugh during the entire flight was wounding.

Outside the window and far below there was nothing but ocean. Sun glinting off the sea was pleasant to look at. Ethan ended his call and looked as well.

"Looks like we're flying south," he observed.

"Excuse me, gentlemen, can I call ahead for anything you might need?" Cindy offered, her voice with a glint of Southern accent. I turned. She was looking at my cleaned but still rough coveralls. "A driver? Lodging? Perhaps clothing?"

"Where're we going?" Ethan asked me.

I laughed. First time in a good while. I guess it was an odd sound. Ethan's bug eyes widened.

"Interesting," he said.

"You know, I've no idea."

◆ ◆ ◆

THE JET landed.

We were warmly greeted on the tarmac by two young men melting in black business suits.

"Welcome to Jalisco."

They held our hands as though we were senile tourists, leading us through customs in the Jet Thru lobby. Outside of the private terminal, there was more of the sticky, sweet, humid air. On the sidewalk, soldiers—boys, really—shouldered black automatic rifles. Their young eyes were distant and blank. And frightening.

The curbside was packed with smoking buses and taxis. Street vendors had set up on the sidewalk, hawking sno-cones and over-cooked tamales. Ethan and I passed.

A black limousine nudged its way aggressively to the curb. Ethan stepped to it. I stood still, looking over its roof. What do you do but grin?

Pauline had somehow arranged to have my very old Jeep, a Willy, delivered. It was parked at the side of a concrete island two lanes over. One of the frightening young soldiers was guarding it. He looked at a photograph twice before offering me the keys.

"My darling Pauline." I took the keys.

"Soon-to-be ex-darling Pauline," Ethan quipped.

I gave him the gaze of death.

I climbed into the Willy. No doors. No top.

"I'll drive," I said. "You'll navigate."

"Where are we?"

I ignored that. "Go inside and get a map."

He did and climbed in beside me a minute later.

"Where are we going?" he asked, starting to unfold the map.

"You know, I've no idea." I handed him my oft-errant cellphone. "Do a search on R."

"I thought you lost your cell?"

"I tried."

He searched the contacts for R.

"Rhonda?" he asked.

"One and only."

"Who is she?"

"Important. Ask her where my house is."

CHAPTER THREE
♦ ♦ ♦

OOPS

FATIMA MOSLEY was at her immense steel desk, in her executive chair, looking through the round portal door Rolf had entered. One of her underlings had brought her the FedEx box with the day's mail. There was a storm gathering outside and the metal plates under her feet groaned. Her office walls were also steel, unpainted. As she had learned over the past three years, metal was a conduit of sound rather than a buffer. Sounds, though muted, carried from all over the studio to her—not voices, but the big sounds, like the lift that raised and lowered film sets to and from storage. This was why she wore furry earmuffs.

A white easel stood at her back and was covered with her handwritten list of planned shows and movies, along with dates and income and expense data. Earlier that day, she had dry-erased *Tin Can* and underlined *Oops*. This was the name of the next three-day shoot. The easel was placed strategically, to block the large office's single round window. She sat under grilling florescent lighting from above.

Her phone rang and she raised an earmuff and answered it with silence, listening to the progress report from the set. After a week of set construction, her film crew were in place and ready. The call ended without her saying a word.

"Won't bother you with the details," Rolf said, standing in front of her desk. "We're a go. We're just waiting for the client."

"Does that mean you want me to get involved?"

"Yes, please. His minders are struggling."

"He's still in the Ye Olde, I assume?"

"Yes."

"Cheez-It," Fatima breathed.

She left her office and walked the narrow halls, her knee clacking along the twisting path to the door of the Ye Olde. She paused before knocking, which was rare. The client was an obscenely wealthy beef exporter from Uruguay, a well-mannered and sickening, vicious man: Señor Tabare Artigas Borda.

"*Meu apologis, mas e' tempo, Señor Borda*," she spoke in her skim-learned Portuguese. Señor Borda's two minders stood inside the door, looking tough, rough, and bored stupid. She then saw that Señor himself wasn't present.

There was no response from inside the Ye Olde. She leaned in and glanced at the casting couch and bed and gymnast bench. No movement or sound except the metal echoes from all corners.

A moment later, a metal hasp inside the room creaked. Across the room, the portal door opened and there was Señor Borda, in costume and theatrical makeup.

Needs a little touch up, Fatima groused to herself.

Señor Borda's eyes were both wide and wild. For the scene remake of *Oops*, the end-of-the-world television series, he had chosen the role of the clan leader and wore the heavy black shoes, filthy cardigan, and forest-green frock dress. Fatima stepped inside and looked past "her" and deeper into the casting room.

The premiere-optioned elderly actor, Dan Marrow, was prostrate on a medical bed in the corner of the room. He was attached to IVs, and his exposed, sagging chest was tagged with monitor stickies. He was clearly in medical distress. It didn't help his demeanor that Señor Borda had clearly had his way with the once-famous lead in a series of '80s espionage films.

As Señor Borda walked up to his handlers, three of Fatima's paramedics stepped past her and went to the aid of the old and frightened and deeply offended actor. Señor Borda's toys were on the floor. While the paramedics worked to calm and treat Dan Marrow, Fatima turned away.

"*Señor Borda, meu apologies,*" she offered. Not knowing the Portuguese, she added in English, knowing one of minders would translate, "I know he was promised, but Mr. Marrow will be unable to appear."

That was going to cost her $400K, but she believed the shoot could be done without Dan—his role was mostly ornamental, the wise, sad sage of the post-apocalypse clan. "Little more than a tree in the background," she muttered under breath.

Señor Borda went out the door with stony silence, his handlers trailing, speaking calming and pacifying Portuguese.

Fatima followed, her artificial knee slowing her efforts to catch up with the "star" in his green dress and old boots. She finally caught up to him as he entered the soundstage, and all the voices changed in tonality, caused by the sound-buffering mattresses bolted to all the walls.

To the left was the massive, darkened movie set for the remake of the pivotal scene in *Dark Liaison*, a vehicle that garnered the star one of those shiny globes and a gold, naked statuette named Oscar. That shoot was ten days out and of no current concern to Fatima. She had *Oops* to get through first. They were scheduled for twenty-six hours of filming to get Señor Borda's five-minute performance completed. And get his amazingly large check cashed.

Fatima followed the star past the tower stage lights and in through the many open and glowing equipment cases, minding her step over the cables that slithered in all directions. The shot was already lighted, and there was marginally controlled chaos among the various crews.

Rolf appeared at her side, juggling two disparate stacks of paper in her arms while tilting her head and taping her headset off.

"And?" Rolf asked.

"Marrow's not gonna make it. Got his stand-in?"

"Yes. We've run one of the older grips through costume and makeup. He's ready. Not much of a semblance but close. Is Borda okay with the stand-in?"

"Has to be. He knew of Marrow's prior medical condition before we did the contract. And his antics in the Ye Olde have caused the current ones. I'll be cutting a Marrow check for four hundred and…"

Fatima didn't finish.

Rolf nodded and tapped her headset. "Get me the DP."

The director of photography was standing seven feet away and took the call. Fatima turned to her next concern: Rose Daiss.

"Cheese an' Christ," she grumbled.

Rose had hit the deck, her obese weight and stumpy legs having misguided her. She had missed her La-Z-Boy by at least four feet and spilled her lunch and lay in Tanqueray and ice and glass, struggling against her aides, who were to trying to assist her up.

"Tell me again why we have a director?" Fatima asked rhetorically.

"Professionalism," Rolf answered.

Fatima barked laughter before saying, "Mm-hmm, was kidding. The clients demand it."

Rolf went into her AD role, calling out, "Quiet, quiet, quiet!"

Fatima crossed to her preferred perch, a good way back from the crews and equipment, standing before the digital feeds on the head-high monitors. The full-screen feeds carried from the three cameras that were already turned on but not filming.

The set was a ruined underground train station. Dust floated and had settled everywhere, on her props and the furniture, the extras who had been poised and standing around stupid and near frozen for a couple of hours. As directed, they all looked disheveled and scared and bewildered—not unlike how they had arrived at the studio. Also on the set were open cooking fires and their battered belongings, mostly dirty blankets and old suitcases.

She watched Señor Borda fawn and deferentially, graciously address the cast as each took up the gaff-taped marks for where they would move from in the first shot. The rehired cast was a happy lot— they had gladly accepted their great big checks; not one had had to be chemically persuaded into appearing. As was always the case, lots of miles had worn out their faces, but they otherwise looked presentable and offered slight resemblance to their former selves. Fatima smiled. The Uruguayan beef tycoon hadn't opted for the all-nude cast off the premium plan menu. The has-been actors' faces were familiar, but gravity had done terrible things to their figures.

The first scene to be reenacted was the discovery of the packing crate of vaccinations in sealed packets. As the star—in this case, Señor Borda in drag—opened the crate and the bewildered and ragged extras moved to see, the well-armed militia would approach. Next up was the start of a bloody confrontation over control of the medicines.

The tall lights on towers filtered through amber plastic screens gave off natural daylight. The lighting combined with professional makeup made Señor Borda beatific.

The cinematographer and director were in a heated argument, Rose Daiss loud and slurring.

"Places!" Rolf bellowed.

Fatima watched the first walk-through.

Her cellphone purred, and she smiled with relief, able to walk away to take the call. Moviemaking was such a slow, tedious process. Hours spent getting a few seconds of pretentious drama.

Entering the shadows away from all the lights and action, she answered the call by tapping the cell and saying nothing.

"Ma'am, this is Chuck. We've got Mr. Marrow calmed, but we're losing him."

"Be right there. Get him his camera," Fatima replied, ending the call. She gazed across the soundstage to the massive darkened set for

Dark Liaison. That shoot was going to be absurdly lucrative and a royal pain in the ass.

The voices and lights and chaos were receding as she crossed to the faintly lit round-topped exit door. She entered the silence of the hallway, the clicking of her knee the only sound as she made her way through the narrow corridors. The triage room was down the hall from the Ye Olde.

Sure enough, there he was, laid out with his feet to the portal window. The paramedics were disconnecting the tubes and wires, and he lay there looking heavily sedated and serene. Fatima fought off the urge to glare at the dying man. He was clearly not the least bit concerned or apologetic about the selfish timing of his death and her loss of the $400K.

Fresh air and rain were coming in through the window, erasing some of the putrid scent of his released bowels. He had an 8mm movie camera on his bony chest, held in long, weak fingers.

A paramedic extracted the oxygen tubes from his mouth and throat, making a sucking and *blopping* sound.

Dan Marrow was ignoring Fatima, which was both rude and irritating. She moved to the medical display and controls.

"Get outta here," she yelled at the three medics in blue gowns.

They departed and she studied the equipment controls, all multicolored lights and meaningless dials.

Then Dan Marrow spoke. Sort of. It was a husk of his former eloquent speech. His bony thumb twitched and pushed the Record button on his 8mm.

"You can turn off my life support now. I'm dying to see what I'm in next."

CHAPTER FOUR

◆ ◆ ◆

PUERTO MITA

NAVIGATING FROM the airport through the next town was a third world nightmare of chaos, two near-death collisions and lots of clogs of all types of vehicular traffic—some of it motorized, most overburdened loads on wheels that happened to have engines. We didn't run anyone over, which was surprising because the cobblestone streets were being used as the town's sidewalks and the sidewalks held crowded food and produce markets.

Ethan had the map and the directions scribbled from Rhonda. He did a fair job of getting us to the outskirts and onto the very narrow two-lane highway. The Willy is ideal in foreign towns; lightweight, narrow tires, easy turning and backing up. One gauge on the dash, a two-lever transmission, and the spare tire mounted on the side, next to Ethan's knee. I think he was glad to have the directions to focus on, because he reached twice for nonexistent seatbelts. We cleared the babble and chaos of the town, and I worked the Willy up through the gears to a refreshing fast clip on the highway. We entered a low running valley—the sides of the road were matching fields of black from crops burning, smoke still spiraling upward. After blasting across the valley, we were under a ridiculously beautiful blue evening sky with orange-dipped clouds over the sea to our right.

I got Ethan's elbow in the ribs and heard him yelp. I looked up and swerved the Willy past a slow-rolling caravan of work trucks.

"Probably best you enjoy the view," I told him and chose to mind the steering. The highway ended and ran along a two-lane that climbed steep into the trees—scratch that, up into the jungle—and the world became a canopy of green. The road twisted through endless, odd-angled, tight turns. I engaged the front-wheel axle for grip and we turned and climbed, turned and climbed, occasionally seeing lights up in the trees from fires and residences.

When darkness fell, it fell fast. Ethan found a flashlight in the glove box and navigated us past a few dead ends and wrong turns, then to the correct address number nailed to a fence post. I turned in and we climbed up the driveway, foliage brushing us. A clearing opened before us, with a turnaround driveway in front of a dark villa that looked like it had barely survived an airstrike or two. I parked on the large chunk gravel. There were two black Mercedes coupes parked further up around the curve. I looked up the wide front steps to the large door, which was open. A swaying lantern light was starting to warm the opening from inside. We climbed out of the Willy, and I retrieved my satchel from the rear jump seat as the light expanded out onto the long landing, revealing its sag to the left and its overgrowth of foliage. I smelled the ripe jungle mixed with the scent of burnt brake discs and transmission oil behind us.

A diminutive man stepped out. He wore a white dinner jacket and shirt, black slacks, and bare feet. Ethan and I climbed the crumbling, uneven steps to the landing, and the doorman with his oil lantern walked back inside. So much for *hola*.

We followed him inside to a cavernous foyer and a great room filled with tired furniture much in disrepair. Overhead vines wove the ceiling, snaking up from the corners of the cracks in the wall and uneven parquet flooring. Critters scampered, and I saw a large iguana take refuge in a tangle of jungle brush at a window along the right wall.

We followed the silent doorman into a long-forgotten ballroom, also filled with suspect furniture. To the left was a once-grand curving staircase, and we followed our guide up the stairs. The landing doors were simple, except the large one at the end. The doorman led us to it and set the lantern down and rolled the big door open. He stepped aside, and Ethan and I entered an entirely new residence.

Electric lamps lit an impressive great room. The air was chilled by silent air conditioning. An elegant dining area was to our left. Before us was a living room of modern leather couches and low tables. To the right was open-air veranda and the shape of a swimming pool defined by torches. Beside it was a library and an open-air office on a raised landing. Wonderful scents of cooking greeted us from the restaurant-sized kitchen beside the dining area, where two women were preparing a meal.

The back of a head of mahogany hair turned around on the middle leather couch before us and there was Sara, looking mischievous and worried and lovely as ever.

"Hey Pierce." She grinned. "Been a good while. Who's the lout you brought along?"

"Hey you. You look good. This is Ethan. Be nice," I said to beautiful Sara. She and I had miles of friendship and a family connection. She was my darling niece's lifelong love.

"I might be. It's up to him. Hello, Ethan."

Ethan was busy taking in the details of the great room.

"I'm Sara," she nudged.

He turned to her and his eyes changed.

I'd seen that look before, the effect of Sara's beauty and intelligent, consuming eyes. I know smitten when I see it.

"Yes, hello, err." He got out.

I laughed.

She rose and circled the couch. Her cocoa body was draped in a loose smock dress.

While Ethan gawked, I said, "The front of this place. Uninviting."

"Intentional," Sara replied. "And a bit of a safety risk, but whaddaya expect? It's a rental. Hungry?"

"Yes. Ethan, Sara is Pauline's *aide-de-camp*—"

"Assistant. Gopher," she cut in.

"A pleasure," Ethan said in dazed voice.

"And you?" She paused before him with her hand out to the dining area. "What do you do besides play Pierce's stunned sidekick?"

"I'm a researcher."

"Oh. Of?" she asked.

Oh boy, I thought, turning to the large table with its crisp white tablecloth and elegant place settings.

"Pauline," I said on his behalf.

"Holy crack, Pierce. You bring along—"

"Not a bio," I said, trying to save Ethan's and my scalps. "He's studying her craft."

Sara's tan pointer finger rose into the air, asking for a pause before she replied. She didn't, and instead led us to the table large enough for twelve, taking the chair across from Ethan with me at her side.

"Do you know you resemble the actress Meg Harry?" Ethan had found his voice, unfortunately.

Oh boy, I thought a second time.

"That's interesting," Sara said. "I don't think I like you."

With that, dinner was served by the two pleasantly smiling women dressed alike the doorman, including bare feet.

The meal was a simple affair. A variety of warm breads and a salad of unusual greens and grilled beef. Fiji water was poured into our glasses. We ate in relative silence—Ethan making discouraged but hopeful attempts to spark conversation on neutral topics. Sara ate with a good appetite and treated Ethan's questions as moths to be brushed away.

"Where's Pauline?" I asked when we were done.

"Still on location."

"Where's the shoot?"

"An island. *Black Island* now—it's the film title."

One of the maids circled the table, asking each of us in turn if there was anything we needed. Ethan asked for an ashtray. I raised an eyebrow, suspecting he'd heard the rumor. Pauline was a collector of them. For years, I scoured bars and bistros for them. No Christmas or birthday present delighted her more. Since 1979, ashtrays have become dinosaurs, but harder to unearth because of their diminutive size. There were many set out among the low tables in the room behind us. The maid brought Ethan one of my last finds, a clear glass oval with orange and brown lettering: "A&W Root Beer." Ethan admired it and didn't take out any kind of tobacco.

"*Black Island*," he said. "Dark and isolated?"

"Yes. She usually comes in on the last boat. Sometimes she sleeps over on location. Dessert, anyone?"

"No thank you, Sara." Ethan spoke her name reverently. "I'd like to be excused and get cleaned up. Wash the travel dust and grime off."

Sara smiled at Ethan for the first time. Well, a half smile.

"Find Señor Brisca—he was the one who greeted you. Have him show you a room. If you like, he can get you a swimsuit. A dive might be more refreshing than a shower."

As though on cue, the big door behind us rolled open and there was our friend, now Señor Brisca, holding an oil lantern. Ethan rose, thanked Sara for the meal, shouldered his haversack, and walked off. I looked to Ethan's setting. The ashtray was gone.

As the door rolled closed, I took out the telegram and unfolded it on the table, then slid it across to Sara. She opened it.

"Yes, she disappeared. We went frantic. But she came back. The filming was on hiatus—cursed good weather rolled in." Sara would have normally smiled at her little joke, but didn't.

"She came back rattled, undone. Spent two nights telegramming your sons. She settled down, settled in, and went back to work, like the professional she is."

"How long was she gone?" I asked.

"Ten days."

"Can have a full life in ten."

"Yes."

"A romantic escape?"

"Could have been. Sorry. But her sending this says no."

Movement out on the veranda caught my eye. A man was out by the pool, in the torchlight. When his face was illuminated, I saw that he was sickeningly handsome. And tall, strong, moving with a big cat's swaying shoulders and walk. He passed under another torch, and I saw his black suit and black shirt, no tie, his opened top button revealing a tan neck and chest. He disappeared from view, possibly making for another door.

Minutes later, the same man made his way casually across the great room to us. Sara slid the telegram to me, and I pocketed it. Instead of turning to the man, she spoke to his footsteps. "He's the studio dick assigned to Pauline."

I looked to him. He wasn't handsome in full light—he was beautiful.

"You're the hubby, right?" he said. "I mean, soon-to-be ex-hubby? I'm Johal. Head of security."

I watched him take a bite of the sandwich he had carried inside. He held it tight in his strong, tan hands.

"Hello Johal, a pleasure, I assume. Can I ask? Shouldn't you be on location?"

He took another bite and stared at me.

"Pauline—"

"Ms. Place," Sara corrected him.

"Pauline," he went on, "asked me to be laid back today. She has a way of saying no."

"Yes." I knew. Miles of marriage and I had heard Pauline say that word no more than a handful of times; scratch that, perhaps three. But when she did, the planets stopped rotating.

"Going to the wharf, Johal," Sara said, making the question a statement.

"Yes." He chewed. And chewed. We watched him until he finished and placed the last bite of crust in the center of Ethan's remaining salad.

"We have another guest?" he asked.

"Yes," Sara told him. "My dear friend Ethan. Now go."

And he did.

When the rolling door closed, Sara looked to me.

"Dessert?"

"Of course." I nodded.

Moments later, we were served shaved ice with an assortment of berries in delicate yellow bowls.

After enjoying the ice and berries, Sara raised her spoon and said, "Come, let's go out back."

We wove through the couches and low tables and lamps and stepped out into the torch-lit night. She sat down at the pool edge and dangled her legs. I sat down beside her and did the same. The pool was empty.

"He could've broken his neck," I said of Ethan.

Sara laughed. "Naw, he would've noticed. And if he didn't, well, would we really want someone that dim around?"

The night air rose from the ocean and gathered jungle flavors and graced and cooled us. A scratchy electric sound came from Sara's pocket. She took out a radio and had a brief conversation in Spanish. My Spanish was rusty. Sara saw my struggle and translated.

"That was the dock crew. She must be sleeping on location. She wasn't on the last boat."

"Hiding from me? No, not her way."

"Time for sleep?" she suggested, and I agreed.

"Señor Brisca will find you a room," she added.

Sara walked alongside me to the big door and stepped back as Señor Brisca rolled it open.

I turned to Sara. She was turning back to the living room.

"I sleep down here on a couch," she said. "Sweet dreams."

Señor Borda led the way along the landing with his oil lantern.

My room was pleasant; large, sparsely furnished, clean, with a private bath and electricity. Setting my satchel on the turned-down bed of fine linen, I waited three minutes after Señor Brisca wished me a good night.

I found Pauline's room after accidently opening Ethan's door and seeing his head and back at his desk. He was lit by the lights from the bathroom and didn't turn around. Pauline's suite had a spacious sitting area before her bedroom door. The furniture was modern and floral scented. The lighting was dimmed to sleepy warm. I crossed to her bedroom door and opened it. There were flowers everywhere—with cards. The balcony doors were closed, and the air conditioning was set to a cool-for-sleep temperature. The room was spotless and relaxed and elegant, and I stood back from the bed, before the couch and table that faced it.

A man's gold-and-blue necktie was draped over the cream leather. I pulled that boxcar of sorrow and regret back to my room.

CHAPTER FIVE
◆ ◆ ◆

THE BARREL

THE BARREL was a roadside service station and diner on a nameless road in a nameless town. Stanley, the owner, was under an elevated automobile in the service bay, bleeding the brakes. He was not above tampering with vehicles to gain repeat business. His wife, Mildred, was behind the bar in the diner, where she served watered drinks to the locals, two old guys at a table sharing a newspaper and arguing. At that moment, she was watching the fat man seated at the counter before her use his half-finished lunch of scrambled eggs and soggy toast to extinguish his cigarettes. Suzi, the whore, was at the end of the bar, talking to her drink. A new face—a traveling salesman—was eyeing her and attempting to chat up anyone whose eyes he could catch. The Barrel had a dusty 1960s décor, the cast wore clothing of that same decade, and the conversations were gibberish, coming from the mouths of the trained monkeys.

◆ ◆ ◆

THE COST of production of The Barrel remake was high—at best a breakeven financially, but Fatima Mosley was okay with that, because the ability to pull off such a difficult shoot for the client would be good PR. In addition, some of the set could be reused because so many television shows took place in bars and diners.

The logistics had been a nightmare. Importing the trainers and the chimps and their cages, which were small portable apartments, had been expensive. The number of retakes required had driven Rose Daiss from the studio in a gin-soaked rage of threats as stagehands rolled her from the soundstage on a gurney. In Rose's stead, the director of photography had been temporarily elevated to director. This decision was a money-saver until a pro could be bought or *persuaded* to join the studio.

As expected, the set was bedlam. The trainers were frazzled and loud. There was the twisted chaos of the chimps in the wardrobe dressing rooms. The catering and dining area was in a constant outrage of bad behavior.

The Barrel's set was lit, but the day was far away from further filming. The various crews were in manic arguments; everyone cursing into the radios and cells. The cast from the last shot left the set, joining the disastrous group lunch with food and plastic cups flying. Some fool had the television show's theme music playing through big speakers, over and over, the melody performed with cymbals and *tinking* piano followed by the sounds of tires skidding and automobiles crashing.

Fatima stood in the soundstage shadows observing all, mentally operating a calculator, figuring the expenses and at times simply staring at was happening in her studio.

Rolf walked to her, a silhouette backlit by the stage lights.

"How's things?" she asked Fatima, tongue-in-cheek.

Fatima's round face crunched inward. She didn't appreciate the wit.

"Where's the client?" she asked.

"The Ye Olde."

Fatima's eyes widened. "Oh no."

"Oh yes." Rolf frowned.

"With who?" Fatima glared at the chimps at the dining table, where the trainers did their ineffective best to calm the cast, to persuade them to settle down.

"Who else? One of the males."

"Call the crew."

"Which one?"

"The Ye Olde. That obscenity will not be filmed. No matter the lost income."

"Yes, we do have standards. Decencies."

Fatima didn't have to look to Rolf to see her expression, see the sarcasm, which was dripping.

"What's our schedule for today?"

"2.59 minutes. The diner counter. The birthday cake scene."

"2.59?"

"Yep. You might've heard, the *director*—" Rolf paused for a fake cough "—has agreed to let the client change his role again."

"Who's out? Who's he in?"

"He wants to be Suzi the whore. Says he has his lines and slurs memorized."

"That's fine. Get Suzi and her trainer paid off and out of my studio."

"One less monkey," Rolf agreed and left the soundstage.

Fatima looked away, to soundstage right, where the complex movie set for *Dark Liaison* stood ready to be rolled into place and warmed up after the current film was done. She heard footsteps and voices approaching from behind and ignored them.

As though reading her thoughts, Mr. Rand, her studio's executive producer, said to her, "That set is a different creature—different challenge."

"Mm-hmm," Fatima acknowledged. "What's our schedule?"

Mr. Rand turned to his new assistant, who held a file open to him. Fatima glanced at both assistants: Asian, *very* young, dressed with edge and fashion. While Mr. Rand scanned the open folder, Fatima asked, "They look like escorts. Are they?"

"Least I'm not fucking monkeys," Mr. Rand replied, not look-ing up.

"That's true."

Another set of footsteps approached; a clumsy clattering of steel-tipped stiletto heels. The client passed by wearing a red spar-kling dress. His face was sickly pale under a tangled, wild wig. His eyes were wild and his lipstick sloppy. Fatima and Mr. Rand watched the client stutter-walk to the lights and noise of the set with a grip guiding him by the elbow.

"You will stay on schedule." It was a statement from Mr. Rand. "We are finally a go with the rest of the *Dark Liaison* shoot."

"Of course. Has the collector's check cleared?"

"The wire transfer was completed, yes," Mr. Rand answered.

"Good. Mm-hmm, that last ten-day shoot was difficult. Has the issue been resolved?"

"I'm confident that it has. Our Miss Pauline Place has come around to having the collector stand in."

"How? This time?"

"We sent her the current addresses for her two sons. With a threat."

CHAPTER SIX

◆ ◆ ◆

VIEWFINDER

I SLEPT with the AC off and the balcony door open. I paid for that choice by waking sticky with sweat, observed by an audience of gnats and lizards and bugs about the room and on my tangled sheets.

"Hey guys." I scowled at the insects and critters as I crossed to the shower through the heavy humid air. Someone had laid an assortment of shorts and large T-shirts on the bath counter. Finding my sizes, I dressed, wondering if the clothing belonged to Johal the goon.

Walking along the dark landing that smelled of mold and jungle rot, I opened the rolling door at the end. Before me, the great room was colorful and clean, filled with bright tropical light.

The different leveled room was empty except the two women in the kitchen. There were voices from out back, in the direction of the brilliant early morning.

Sara and Ethan sat side by side at an umbrella table on the right side of the pool, near where water gushed into the deep end. Two workers were dismantling a low scaffolding, and a third was carrying tools up the steps. They'd been repairing cracks in the gunite. Sara and Ethan appeared to be playing nice-nice with each other, sharing a platter of fruits and breads.

I took the side chair out of the shade and basked in the familiar feel of sun on my skin. I had a pallor from three years of Packard restoration. There was a straw bucket of iced Fiji bottles, and I opened one, sipped, and closed my eyes, content to listen in on those two. Sara and Ethan's voices were quick and energetic. The talk was of the Mamet and Macy schools of acting. I was impressed by Ethan's detailed understanding *and* his having engaged Sara's interest. The talk was argumentative and in depth, and she was holding in the reins of her sharp tongue.

I opened my eyes and peeled and ate a banana. I noticed something different in my recently acquired travel buddy. He was wearing a new pair of dark pince-nez. He shared the chair with his haversack. I smiled, wondering what he was going to pinch this morning. There was a heavy art deco brass ashtray beside the umbrella post, and I put money on it being gone soon. Ethan was sweating profusely and a bit pink in the cheeks.

"Hold that idea," Sara shushed him before nicely adding, "Please."

I arched an eyebrow at that as she rose from the table and circled the pool to the outdoor shower. Twisting a lever, she stepped into the downpour of cool water, unmindful of her clothing. She returned to the table soaking wet and asked Ethan, "Continue, please."

"Her *as if* efforts, her natural ease in the Practical Aesthetics school *isn't* noticeable—that's her daring, her personal *will* appearing."

Clearly he was talking about Pauline.

"It's more than the *will*, it's her commitment, her *pursuit* of action with what the cast is…"

I wanted to cut in on this and ask about Pauline, here and now, but chose to let them chase their tails a bit longer.

My years with Pauline and the miles of similar conversations had interested me at a distance. Theory was fine and somewhat interesting and irrelevant in her case. None of it swayed my unspoken belief that Pauline was a simple, perfect spirit of curiosity. In other words, genuine; a natural.

I opened a second Fiji and watched Ethan rise in mid-conversation and continue to argue with Sara over his shoulder. He walked to the outdoor shower. When he stepped fully clothed into the cool water, I leaned over and lifted the canvas cover of his haversack and peered inside.

"Nick anything new?" Sara laughed.

"You've noticed?" It was rhetorical.

"Bet it's a compulsion. And at least he's not swiping cars and yachts."

I was familiar with the obsession, having worked on the *Klepto* film in 2011.

"We were given psychological studies to read," I said. "As though that would make my Steadicam operate differently…"

"And?"

"Can we talk about Pauline now?"

"Sure, but *more* first."

"It's not personal gain. If you saw the film *Klepto*, if anyone saw *Klepto*, it was the president's wife doing the worst of the thefts. Most of them can afford whatever they pinch. It's a disorder. I'd put money on there being a medicinal solution, like everything these days."

I stopped looking and rummaged through the haversack. Ethan was busy circling in the shower and shampooing. There were his Moleskine notebooks, a high-tech radio device, and an assortment of odd stolen items; some I recognized, and some were new. I held up the radio or phone or whatever it was.

"Lemme see," Sara chirped.

"No. Talk to me about my wife."

She ignored my plea. "It's a satellite phone. Can call anyone from anywhere."

A quick glance across to Ethan showed him struggling with the cap of a bottle of cream rinse. I stirred some more inside his haversack. Pressed to the bottom was a silver swan hood ornament from a Packard, like those at Gustin's Restoration.

"Boy was thorough," I said, looking over to Ethan.

"To answer your question…" Sara said. She was also watching Ethan, who was rubbing his head in the shower stream.

"Johal radioed," she told me. "He took the morning boat over. Says all is okay."

"I'm starting to wonder why I'm here."

Ethan's fancy phone began to buzz. Sara eased it back inside his bag.

"I wish I knew more. At least she returned safely. From wherever she went."

"Yes."

Another phone began to ring.

"Mine," Sara said to me and "Yes?" to her cell.

I watched her listen and watched her react—the confident and sure-footed Sara began to look anguished. I was aware of Ethan sloshing into the chair between us, and I leaned forward to look past him.

It looked painful for Sara to listen without commenting, but I don't think she could if she wanted. She turned and stared at me and nodded her chin to the cadence of the voice on the other end. I was aware of Ethan working his hands inside his haversack and ignored him. Sara ended the call with, "Of course," said softly, sadly.

She and I stared at one another for a pause.

"What's wrong?" I asked.

"Pauline has disappeared again. Midshoot. No one knows where or how."

Ethan scraped his chair back and walked away, talking to his satellite phone.

"How far is this island—no, how can I get there?" I asked. My body and face were chilled and flush at the same time.

It looked like Sara wanted to simply stare. Forever.

I dug my phone out.

"There are two boats a day." Sara's voice sounded like it had come through a fog.

I turned my phone on.

"What're you doing?" Sara asked.

I ignored her and stood and walked to the house, selecting R from my contacts.

"Hi, Pie," Rhonda answered. "How's tricks? While I got you, I snooped Pauline's accountants—didja know she's been selling homes?"

In my prior life, my prior complex, dreamy, cinematographer life, Ms. Rhonda had been my studio conduit for inside information as well as coordinator of Pauline's and my schedules. She was also what's known as a *fixer*. All my ties with the studio had been severed, but we had stayed in contact. She was a very good friend and was also brilliant at getting me out of binds.

"I didn't know. I've got a problem."

"Of course.

"Pauline's disappeared."

"Again? Okay. Whatcha need?"

"I need to get to the location."

"Hold a second." I heard the rustling of bedding and a male voice complain.

"Got it," she said. "Black Island. New name for it, courtesy of movie money. It's a small island, a three-mile rock—no matter. Let me check..."

I entered the house while Rhonda clicked on a keyboard.

"It's troublesome. There's a bunch of detail in the location-planning files about tides and reefs. Can't just swing by, Pie."

"Can I fly in? Rent a plane?"

"No. The airfield isn't up yet. Studio's building it after production. Figures. Part of the restoration to pay off the locals."

I went up to my room and pulled on my boots and grabbed my satchel. Rhonda was clicking furiously and muttering, both to herself and whoever was in her bed.

"Got a boat?" she asked.

"No. All I've got is a Willy."

Rhonda laughed, which took a little of edge off my near-panic. "Yes, Pauline had me arrange that. Want a boat?"

"Yes. I can't wait until the night boat."

"'Kay. Where are you?"

"I'm in my bedroom."

"'Kay, walk to the window."

"'Kay," I mimicked.

"See the sea?" she said, then repeated the words. I could hear the smirk.

"Yes. A *lovely* ocean view." I let some edge in. "Rhonda—"

"Well, there you go. You will have to navigate yourself down to the harbor. Want directions?"

"No. Well, maybe. But you're not making sense."

"Pie, get your rear down to the wharf. I'll call ahead."

"Gonna help me steal a boat?"

"No, love. Her boat is there."

I was downstairs, crossing the creepy, dark ballroom before the foyer and front door.

"The *Viewfinder*'s here?"

"Yes—that's how she got there. It's too big for the atoll dock. Something about heft and depth. Dunno."

I fished the Willy keys from my satchel and climbed in behind the wheeling, seeing that one of the two Mercedes were gone. Johal the likely wife thief at the wheel?

"The boat's crewed lightly, Pie."

"How lightly?" I asked. In years past, I had a lot of fun playing skipper of Pauline's boat, but I was about as nautical as a 1948 Packard Model 2293 Station Sedan.

"Lightly as in one. A mechanic rebuilding something and, hopefully, keeping the locals at bay. At bay—ha. I'm sharp this morning."

I steered the Willy around the curved drive and started down the hill.

"Directions, please," I said.

"Go downhill. When you see the waves, turn left."

"Thank you."

"My pleasure. Go find your darling. I'll see what I can do to hire you a full crew. Bye for now."

I drove through dense jungle on dirt and gravel roads, feeling very lost, but kept choosing turns that ran downhill. Sometimes they worked. One led to my making a U-turn beside a pig farm. Thirty minutes later, I smelled the ocean. A narrow, paved road ran between fish-packing buildings and warehouses. This was not your scenic, by-the-sea, quaint fishing village—this was the rundown and impoverished third world of small houses without electricity and wild dogs and people looking at me like I was either lunch or a source of income. There was the smell of fish and fish guts long past their shelf life, and the shore wasn't white sand, but rocky and alive with scavenger birds. As instructed, I turned left and didn't sideswipe any of the long trucks parked before closed doors of unlabeled shops. The wharf came into view.

My cell purred. I was surprised it worked here and stopped the Willy. I was looking at five soldiers and as many bedraggled locals talking and standing in a low stir of dust on the sidewalk, all glaring at me. I decided to keep moving, so I tapped the cell and steered cautiously around the little crowd.

"Pierce? You left something behind," Sara said.

"Yes. Sorry about that."

"What should I do with it? He's entertaining himself in her archives and library."

"Feed him and let him play."

"Sure."

"And thank you."

She ignored that. "Just find her."

"I've got to get to her first."

◆ ◆ ◆

LOOKING THROUGH the masts and radar poles of the decrepit fishing boats, I saw the *Viewfinder* moored in the harbor sixty yards from shore. The mooring made sense; the clean leisure craft must look like a tasty morsel to anyone with a criminal mind. The boat's white lines with teak accents contrasted with the other boats tied off before me on the gray, sunbaked dock. She looked sea worthy.

I parked the Willy out of sight as best I could, in the shade of a Jacaranda tree, hoping that when I saw it again, it wouldn't be a shell elevated on cinder blocks.

The short wharf was a nightmare of worn boards, rusted everything, and low, hostile clouds of flies above smears and chunks of fish meat that trailed from the transoms of the boats, all unmanned. I walked the boards with my chin up, my nose closed, and my eyes on the clean and lovely *Viewfinder*. I didn't see anyone on board.

Zipping up my satchel as I came to the last encrusted boards, I removed my boots, laced them together, and draped them around my neck, trying to remember if the satchel was waterproof.

"Think not," I said, and dove.

The harbor water was warm, I'll give it that, but also toxic with diesel fuel and oil and sewer runoff. After I surfaced, I wiped my face and swam with my head above the water. In years past, a side ladder would be out on the *Viewfinder*, but this wasn't the kind of place you left out welcomes like that. I swam to the transom and climbed up onto it above the twin props.

"Coming aboard," I called up. I seemed to recall that there was a formal way of requesting permission to board. I wasn't concerned with protocol, but I also didn't want to get shot by anyone who might be guarding Pauline's sixty-foot boat.

I waited for a response and got none. I climbed—struggled, to be honest—up the transom and over the rail and onto the polished boards of the stern deck. The *Viewfinder*, familiar from years of joy and family and leisurely adventures, greeted me with silence and secured salon doors.

"Hello," I called. Nothing.

"I'm Pierce Danser. Ms. Place's husband." No reply.

I placed my boots on the deck, opened the satchel, and poured nasty water from it. No movement or voices from behind the salon doors or the railed walkways to the bow. By Hollywood standards, the *Viewfinder* was a small boat, tiny in comparison to the city-sized monoliths owned by many of Pauline's peers. I took out my wet cellphone and tapped it and was greeted with dead.

I would have to wait and see if Rhonda was able to get me a crew. Sitting there dripping on the fine boards, I tried to recall how to raise anchor, how to fire the engines, how to navigate the narrow rock-lined harbor and, oh, how to find an island out there in what I *did* know was an unforgiving, uncaring ocean.

"Is this despondent?" I asked the view, testing the emotional description. If so, it was mixed with worry. And frustration. A nagging interior voice chanted, *Great plan. Great action. You're on it.*

"Thanks," I shouted in sarcasm, trying to negate that useless, but honest, voice.

"You're welcome," a woman shouted back, followed by, "I called Sara. Says you're good."

The voice wasn't from the locked salon doors. I wiped oily water from my face and traced the sound upward.

She was sitting sideways on the flying bridge helm chair, removing a pair of headphones, looking down at me. All I could see of her was sun-streaked, caramel hair, an interesting, butterscotch face, and her black Ray-Bans. And a one-sided smile. She wore an ice-white ball cap with no logo.

"I'm Walton," she called down in a voice both direct and pleasant. "And you're Pierce the ex, right?"

It wasn't a question, but an affirmation.

"Soon to be, yes," I called back.

She raised a clear thermos filled with ice and sipped. She used the straw.

"You need a crew." It almost sounded like a question.

"Yes," I said. "A few would be good."

"I'm all you get."

"Can you?"

"No. Not until I finish with carburetor number one. Wanna hear?"

Instead of waiting for my reply, she swung around to the helm and cranked the ignition. I heard the start of one of the twin Chryslers—deep and strong. Then the unfamiliar choke and gag of the second engine. I felt the vibration under my rear and stood up. She killed the engines, and I climbed the ladder to the flying bridge.

"Made yourself at home," I said, standing on the square teak landing. In the space forward of the helm, there was a cot with a folded linen sheet and portable mosquito netting, as well as an ice chest, a rifle, two wooden boxes of food, and a lantern. At the foot of the cot was an open canvas carry-all with neatly folded clothing made of sheer fabrics. All were bright primary colors or detailed floral.

She was watching me, studying me behind those black shades with her head tipped, as though done with my face and considering my physique. She stood and scooted over onto the second helm chair, offering me the first. I wanted to see the eyes that came with that lovely mouth and thin, fine nose.

Sitting down beside her, I watched her hands on the radio and radar dials. Her small, strong fingers were nicked and cut and smeared with black grime. I looked at my own. They were clean but equally marred by work with tools and metals.

"Where do you want to go?" she asked.

"I need to get to the film set."

"I can do that."

"When? Today?"

"Wanna hear that carb again?"

I shook my head. She responded with winning grin.

"I'm hoping the parts arrive soon."

"Soon? As?"

"I was promised today. Might be Christmas. This sad, backward country. Tell me, do you see ghosts?"

"I'm sorry?"

"Memory haunts. On the boat?"

"I *could*, yes."

"Embrace 'em," she said kindly, lowering her gaze to the helm electronics.

"Can we rebuild the carburetor?" I asked.

"I bet we could, but my instructions are to never repair, only replace parts."

"My wife is missing."

"Well, then let's get to work. Noticed your hands—you do real work?"

"Yes. I rebuild Packards."

"Oh? Any specific era?"

"The '46s through '56."

"The new ones," she said with a laugh. "And you're married to a movie star?"

"Not for long." I was starting to enjoy her quick, twisting thoughts.

She handed me a familiar ring of keys and said, "Let's go below. Grab the charts."

I pocketed the keys and grabbed the charts from the tube on my side of the helm. She followed me down the ladder and stood with her face to the sun as I fumbled to find the salon key.

Walton went in first, taking the charts from under my arm and crossing through the comfortable, spotless salon to the dining table. She unrolled the three charts, placed four of Pauline's ashtrays out to hold them flat, and took out the old Chrysler manual.

Looking around, I did sense a few ghosts. Pauline and me. My dead brother Jared and me, goofing off and drinking, thinking we were quite the wits. The salon and the forward galley were once places of love and delight.

"You're looking kind of weepy." Walton nudged me from the reverie. "Get us the toolboxes."

"Okay," I agreed. "You don't sleep inside the boat?"

"Easier to protect it from high ground."

"Right," I agreed. I went and opened the hatch to the engines and climbed down. The toolboxes were just inside, next to the engines.

"We'll need the lights," I called back, and just like that, Walton threw the breakers. She climbed down in beside me and we scrunched close. It was clear movement would be tough, awkward at best.

"Tell you what, handsome," she said, "go to the lower helm and let me work."

Over the next two hours, I utilized all my mechanical expertise learned from the Packard work by turning the lower helm ignition key whenever Walton called out to me.

We broke for lunch and agreed to eat outside rather than the dining area. Up on the flying bridge, we were blessed with a southern wind that brushed away some of the humidity and smells from the docks and buildings just across the water.

I extended the Bimini over the helm and we ate in its shade. She handed out a lunch of tortillas, unlabeled bottled water, and a local greasy white cheese that she enjoyed and I held suspect, but didn't comment on. Or taste. Either for my benefit or because we had shade, Walton removed her sunglasses and I had an *oh Lord* moment. Her eyes were intelligent and quick and lovely. She turned them straight to me and half smiled, mysteriously, before looking forward to the harbor mouth to the sea.

"Isla de Marionettes isn't far," she said, and I learned the name of what I knew as Black Island.

"Let's get back at it," she said. We climbed down, and I took my important position at the lower helm with the key at the ready while Walton climbed into the engine compartment. Our new partnership morphed into that of a tedious married couple, both of us yelling to one another. Over the next three hours, Walton's voice got edgier and mine grew soft, almost cowering. She vented her frustration with the carburetor seals, revealing her pirate's mouth.

"Wanker!"

"You useless hole!"

"Stubborn quim!" was my favorite, even though I had no idea what that was. Better her ranting at the carburetor than me.

"Cut it," she shouted, and I turned off the engines as she climbed out of the compartment. She appeared beside me, sweaty and smudged, with a wrench in her hand. One glance at her clenched expression told me it was not the time for wit.

"I need a rinse. Getting too angry," she said. She left the salon, and I heard her climb to the top bridge. A minute later she came back inside, walking past me through the galley and into the short hall. The bathroom door click-locked behind her and the shower started.

When Walton reappeared, she was wearing khaki shorts over a one-piece floral swimsuit. Her hands were scrubbed, her tan skin shiny, and, thankfully, the smile had returned. True, it was a bit sideways, but it was clear the shower had been a good choice.

"Better," she said. "I'm back on earth."

She called to shore for ice and food, speaking in fluent Spanish. That done, her second call was to the carrier service. After a few minutes of being polite and patient, she let loose.

"Sod that! I need the parts yesterday, you—" She restrained her tongue, which was a shame. I wanted to hear what the next colorful slur was. She ended the call without success.

"Seals are now good, but the pump jet and injection tube…," she told me. "Those can't be repaired. We have to wait for the replacement carb."

A raggedly dressed boy in a row boat rowed over dinner and ice. Walton put the side ladder in place and together we hefted the wooden box and ice bags.

"Pay him, please," she said.

I took out my soggy wallet, guessed two US twenties would do. The boy's eyes lit up, and he climbed down fast, the cash pushed deep in his pocket.

It was nearing sunset. Both the humidity and heat were dropping.

"Believe we're clean enough for the galley table," she said.

She rolled the charts up, while I set out the meal. She ate with a merry gusto; I ate with caution. Later, we sat up out on the stern deck enjoying iced water and the fading heat of the gold sun sinking into the rocks that lined the harbor.

"The parts might come tonight," she reassured me. "Or in the morning."

There was an hour of some kind of unpleasant ruckus across on the pier; shouts and pleas and orders. And then quiet again. Neither of us turned to watch.

"I have to crash," Walton told me. Her fingertips touched my wrist. I looked down to her small, strong hand on my skin.

"Thank you for the tolerance," she added. "I'm good at what I do, but don't play well with roadblocks."

"I've learned." I smiled.

"Get some sleep," she said and headed off to sleep up on the flying bridge.

I sat listening to her climb the ladder and settle in up above. I drank ice water and watched the evening dissolve into night, twice refreshing the ice and water from inside. I was in no rush to go make a bed on the salon couch. I had already decided to not take up the stateroom bed or the bunks in the short hall. Through all those doors were memories of love, of Pauline and our two sons.

"Like ghosts."

I recall saying that when I went finally went inside. As I laid down on the couch, there was a spiral of regrets waiting to expand and twist and keep me awake all night. Sometimes the past can be greedy that way. To what good besides to stall us out? Breathing deep and calm, I sank slowly, but I still went under, into a deep sleep.

◆ ◆ ◆

WE WERE both up at dawn, Walton back at work down in the engine compartment with me trying to help. There were two open parts boxes propping the compartment door open. The parts had been rowed across in the night. I listened to her converse with herself and the engine while trying to help. After three hours, she raised her steady, lovely eyes and winked.

"Ta-da."

Climbing out, she crossed to the helm with her hands in an oily rag, turned the key, and both engines purred into life.

"Well done," I told her. "What can I do?"

"I'm hungry," she said.

I went to the galley and took two cans of soup out of the food box from the night before and foraged for a can opener. We ate tepid soup and drank water. She sat at the helm, drinking soup from a cup while testing the engines at various RPMs.

"Raise the anchors," Walton said finally, listening to the purring engines.

Five minutes later, we were trolling to the harbor mouth. We both were on the lower bridge, with the marked-up charts on the table. The town rolled away behind us to the left. There were swells but no waves at the harbor exit. Walton cleared it and turned the *Viewfinder* north. The helm radio was on and she chatted with other skippers, mostly in Spanish. It all sounded like friendly banter and numbers to me. She set the throttles to a cruising pace and engaged the autopilot and left the helm.

"Well done," I told her.

I received a grin and a nod as she took up the binoculars and aimed them north. My thoughts focused on the unknown Black Island and my missing wife, no matter our status. First thing to do when on shore was to find out who was in charge of the search. From there, figure out how I could best help.

◆ ◆ ◆

IT WAS supposed to be a two-hour trip, but Walton backed off the throttle at the halfway point, frowning to the windshield.

"You're going to need a slicker," she said.

I looked to the north and saw it. A gray wall of bad weather was in our path. The sea out before us was clear and blue and nearly calm. Not so a couple of miles further. I knew from long ago how quickly the idyllic can change to drenched and scary and cold. I went and pulled on a yellow slicker from a locker. Walton already had hers on. She chewed a tortilla and I sat beside her at the helm while she talked to other boats. The storm from the north was scrolling fast to us on the radar.

The winds kicked up. Minutes later, the waters were a boiling chaos. The *Viewfinder* climbed swells turned gray with menacing white crests. The bow rode up wave faces and back down the other side, white water rushing the walkways along both sides of the bridge. Walton worked the throttles and wheel with calm expertise, keeping us indirectly going north, making progress, while also protecting the boat.

"Seen worse," she said at some point.

I wished I could say the same.

After forty-five minutes of rough seas, she raised the binoculars.

"There it is," she said.

I looked. I squinted. I stared. I accepted the offered binoculars.

Some ten minutes later, we were two hundred yards off the island, such as it was. Even with the clouds and distance and rain, I could tell this wasn't your tropical tourist's wet dream. This was a long wall of cliffs with short green grass across the ridges.

Walton slowed for a safe approach. I scanned the island for any sign of light and manmade structures. There were none. The best that could be said about the island was that it was blocking us from the full brunt of the northern storm.

"You're going to have to dinghy in," Walton said. She looked sad on my behalf. Bringing the boat to within a hundred yards offshore, she idled the engines.

"How do you make a movie on a rock?" she asked. "Don't see a harbor or beaches."

"Copters?" I answered. "Did this once before. Another island, another film, years ago."

"Working with your wife?"

"No, we rarely worked together. In the other life, I was good with the cameras."

"You made movies?"

"No—well, I was a cameraman."

"That's interesting, I think. Good prep for working on Packards, I'm guessing." She said this last deadpan. We both shared a smirk.

"I'm stopping here," she said. "To protect the boat. Might drop an anchor. I'll watch the seas and storm and decide."

"You're going to stick around?"

"Long as I can. Don't forget your bag."

"Everything in it is shot," I said, looking at my satchel on the couch.

"I restocked it."

I shouldered it and followed her out onto the aft deck. Seeing the angry, confused swells was intimidating. I looked across the hundred yards to the cliffs. The rain had darkened the rocks to deep gray. The cliffs were steep and uninviting.

Together, we took up the tether line and pulled the trailing dinghy to the transform platform. I looked again to the coast, not moving any closer to the stern rail.

"Is this the best location?" I asked.

"Actually, yes. Chart shows a small cove—"

"All I see is cliff."

"It's deceiving. As you get closer, you'll see the turn in."

"Are you sure?"

"I'm not, but the chart is."

"I hope God loves chart makers."

We were both soaked and being knocked about by the winds. I wiped rain from my face as Walton aimed the binoculars to shore, her tan finger adjusting the focus dial. I was stalling, watching her and ignoring the stern rail and the dinghy down below. The *View-finder* listed hard to port from another swell. I thought of simply standing there forever, watching her watch the island.

She lowered the field glasses and considered my gaze.

"What?" she asked. "Why are you looking at me like that?"

Walton the lovely, the focused, the distant.

Her eyes read my expression while I searched for true words.

"Don't," she said to me. "Get to work, married man."

She turned and spat rain water. How does a woman do that and look adorable?

"Right." I looked away and moved to the rail.

She had placed the stern ladder, which made the climb down easier. I lowered into the dinghy, which was little more than an inflated donut with an engine. Keeping my gaze turned from the coast, I focused on starting the outboard. Walton tossed the tether line and it landed across my knees. The engine started with the first pull. I gathered in the line before engaging the prop. The metal clamor of the fast-idling engine was loud and rattled me. I finally looked across to the shore, such as it was, and shivered and blamed that on the rain.

A swell tipped the dinghy aggressively, and I caught my balance before being spilled out. Putting the prop in gear, I steered away at a cautious pace from the big boat. There was a hundred yards of cruel and hungry sea between me and that gray rocky coastline.

Forty yards in, I still saw no signs of the alleged cove. I did see birds flying and landing along the cliff wall, doing what helicopters couldn't. Refocusing, I hoped that God *adored* chart makers.

CHAPTER SEVEN

◆ ◆ ◆

MR. C

FATIMA SAT at the middle of the dining table in the screening room with Rolf to her left and Mr. Rand on her other side. The three of them meeting to put their heads together. And eat.

Same meal, same food, every day. Tureens of spaghetti with meat sauce and side bowls of meatballs had been set before Fatima, who did the serving. Mr. Rand sat a way back from the table, his meal untouched, watching his boss eat with a relentless gusto, talking as she chewed, splattering the white linen with red sauce and bits of errant meat. He buttered a roll, watched her full fork slide into her eager mouth, set the roll down and took a sip of the chocolate milk that was also a constant at the dinner meetings. Her studio. Her menu. He turned away and stared at the big blank screen on the opposite wall and gave Rolf his ears.

"Yes, she's late. Delayed. Can't change the weather."

"How hostile is she?" Fatima asking, drinking from her glass.

"Very."

"Mm-hmm. How's my film set?"

"Production is ready. Everything's ready."

"Got every last monkey off my ship?" Fatima chewed and sprayed.

Mr. Rand widened his eyes at that. The boss rarely referenced the fact that the studio—her studio—was on a self-contained trawler.

"Yes, of course. Only critters are the rats with long tails."

"Okay. How's our co-star?"

"Spitting nails."

There was a knock on the metal door. Fatima looked up from her fork and plate.

"There he is now, I bet. He demanded a visit."

The metal door to their left groaned, being opened by a new face—the travel aide of the collector. The aide stepped back, and Mr. Rand also groaned, albeit into his napkin. Rolf stood, and Fatima paused with her full fork before her wide open mouth.

The collector was in costume, such as it was, a slight bathing suit, the front of which rose, indicating his anticipation. His skin below the chest had the color and texture of an uncooked chicken; from the chest bone up, all the skin was horribly disfigured. He appeared to have been dunked upside down in boiling oil, long ago. His round head was barren of hair except for sprouts of straight black shoots. His eyes were way too round, because his eyelids were gone.

"I'm hearing that my co-star isn't here yet," he said by way of greeting.

"Mr. Deung—oh. My apologies—Mr. C," Rolf stumbled.

"Can it, lesbo," the collector said. "Is it true?"

Rolf stopped in her tracks halfway to him and his aide.

"She's delayed, but en route," Fatima smoothed and added, "The weather."

"Don't give a *frip* about the weather," the collector cut her off. His voice was also disfigured due to the absence of lips and the damage to his tongue.

Mr. Rand was more than done with dining. He stood up, buttoned his expensive suit coat, and put on a professional smile.

"Mr. C, we are on schedule. May I walk with you to makeup, sir?"

"That would be fine," the collector agreed, getting the words out without mangling them. He addressed Mr. Rand with his plate-round eyes staring at Fatima.

"I'll go on ahead and make sure they're ready. For our star," Rolf chimed in. She walked past the collector, giving him a wide berth.

Looking sad, Fatima set her fork down and began to rise.

Mr. C shook his head at her and said with deep sarcasm, "Enjoy."

Mr. Rand stepped to the collector's side and offered his hand. The collector had a known penchant for hand holding and extended his own. The two men turned.

Fatima took up her fork as her radio buzzed. She took a bite and answered.

"Copter's a mile off," came through within waves of static.

She didn't reply. Instead she looked at her meal. She laid her linen napkin on the food like lowering a shroud, frowned, stood, and headed out the second other door.

◆ ◆ ◆

FATIMA ENTERED the soundstage, middeck down in the bowels of the trawler, and passed The Barrel set, which was centered on the platform elevator and ready for storage. She started across to the film set, which was much grander in scale and complexity due to being for movies instead of television. The crews had also doubled in size, and many faces had changed. The set was glowing under the heat and false daylight provided by the six scaffold and low set lights that circled the cameras and crews. Unlike the television productions, these people were quiet enough that she could hear the click release of her knee.

"Oil that," the collector had advised without invitation when he first came aboard. The man was as subtle as piranha.

"I like the sound—it reminds me," she had replied sweetly, regardless of her desire to see *his* knees enter her Make-A-Bait in the stern room.

"Of what?" he asked before shaking his head. He knew. Everyone knew. The incident had been splashed in detail in the trades and celebrity rags. A high-speed crash. Another DUI. Two drugged, underage, male prostitutes in the back, both battered in the accident. Charges dropped with a promised thirty-day detox and studio persuasion.

She walked closer to the set, the sound of her knee barely audible. The set itself was simple, a double-sized, claw-footed bathtub in a candlelit library. The candle flames gave a warm contrast to the white porcelain tub and the rich wood tones of the bookcases. She recalled the set design notes and clips and photographs from the original *Dark Liaison* film, and the gussy artistic babble about shades of chocolate, including white.

The scene itself was a large part of the reason Pauline Place had earned both a Globe and an Oscar, some seventeen years before. In it, her character was going to finally submit by seducing the adoring and mad cleric—it would be their first bath together and their final goodbye.

"Twenty-three million will get ya almost anything," Fatima muttered. Soon the wealthy burn ward bully and the much older star were going to do a remake.

And there was the chicken skin, half-cooked co-star now, being coddled onto the set by Rolf and crew. He moved into the full throw of the defused stage lighting. This did nothing appealing to his appearance. The twenty-five members of the film crew were milling about the set, and the cranes, trestles, dolly cameras, and tool and equipment bays. Most were talking into headsets and referencing their notes in binders. Fatima looked away, frowning. The differences between television and moviemaking production was narrowing, but there was still the contrast in scale. Make a movie and you suddenly needed an army of insects. Well-paid insects at that.

Her radiophone purred on her wide hip and she tapped it and leaned her ear unnecessarily to her headset. She didn't greet the caller or speak. It was a brief piece of important information.

"She's a mile off."

Tapping the radio off, she entered the darkness of the soundstage shadows, and scowled. Exiting through a side doorway, she headed for the stairs and climbed.

"Gonna burn out this knee," she muttered between breaths, reaching one level and beginning the climb to the next. The steel walls added a faint echo to her ratcheting knee.

She was met topside by three ship crew members, each looking serious and surprised to see the studio head, who rarely left her cocoon down below. Fatima squinted at the sliding door to wild gray storm outside. Out on the wind and rain, the helicopter was lowering slowly and tentatively to the helipad. Several crew members moved out for it.

When the copter's tires met the deck, the men went into quick professional action, temporarily securing the copter with cables and blocks. The rotors continued to spin, but slowed. The side door was opened, and the steps came down.

Two big men stepped down, heads lowered, the spinning wind and rain washing them. They stopped at the base of the steps and looked back.

A third man appeared. Johal. With *her* on his arm. He looked a bit uncertain, but not Pauline Place. She came down the stairs looking straight at the door between herself and Fatima. She and Johal crossed the deck; he was looking about and shouting to her. She never turned nor acknowledged anyone from the helicopter steps to the sliding door into the ship.

Fatima didn't speak at first—she studied. The actress was shaking—but only her hands. As soon as she was inside, she pulled on a pair of shades, covering her famously beautiful eyes, but not before Fatima saw that the woman wasn't frightened. She was shaking with rage. The door closed, and in the instant quiet, those black shades aimed right at Fatima's head. Fatima almost took a step back, but commanded herself to keep her place.

Tall and handsome Johal helped the actress from her rain coat. The actress allowed this without changing her deadly expression, lips pulling back a touch, revealing perfectly white, hungry teeth.

"Welcome to—" Fatima said and faltered, which was rare. Those black glasses were drilling right through her—no, inside her. Boring a hole into the nest of her fears.

CHAPTER EIGHT

◆ ◆ ◆

ISLA DE MARIONETTES

I IMAGINED that the cove was the size of a kitten's tongue on the table-sized island chart. When it first appeared along the wall of cliffs, it looked like little more than a dent. Walton had sent me out at high tide. The splash and swells were mostly blocked, and I bobbed with the engine cut, staring at the gray rock face. All I had to do was clamber from the dinghy and climb about twenty feet of rain-slick rocks. I sat and stared, frightened and uncertain.

"Action," I called. I scoffed at the old filmmaking command, but it was also true. Sometimes our best choice is to simply propel ourselves forward. Sure beat staying aboard the rubber donut and contemplating my fears.

A swell lunged the dinghy into the rocks to my left, and I reached out in vain. The next wave was larger and smashed the dinghy hard. I was afraid that the rocks might cut and deflate the dinghy, so I lunged with the tether line in one hand and my satchel on the other shoulder.

I got a firm grip on rock as the swell retreated. Pulled myself out of the dinghy.

My grasp failed me. I slipped and scratched on the rocks and splashed into the water, going under. The water wasn't cold, but it was angry and worked me over—my knees smacked against rocks. I was spun around, and my hip struck a rock, setting off a flare of pain. Still underwater, my boot toe connected with rock, and I pushed off, surfacing just in time for the next wave to wash over, slamming me forward. I let go of the tether and used my hands and feet to find anything to hold on to. I knew just enough to not look back, not look up, but focus on every split and outcropping my boots and hands could use. I never fell. I never looked up, never looked down, but fought for slow and steady progress. I searched for handholds and toeholds and climbed, often with the side of my face against the stones wet with rain and slick with white streaks of guano. My hands felt like that had become strong *devices* void of skin and sensitivity. I only paused when sea winds knocked me around. Falling would surely kill my rattled spirit.

The side of my face was scraped, and my teeth were chattering when I saw a patch of low green weed. I didn't let relief overwhelm me, but worked myself up onto the level. Standing before me a few yards away was a flock of birds with turquoise webbed feet. They looked like half penguins, half ducks. I stared at them as I crawled across the rocks and grass and away from that cliff. I knew I should stand, but it still felt safer and saner to keep my body pressed flat until I was a safe distance from the drop to the sea. I crawled until the rocky level had worked my chest and knees over good.

It was nice to have an audience, a welcoming crowd. Hundreds of seagulls and the blue-footed boobies were watching me and thankfully not smirking. But they were calling out—the gulls feigning interest with *gawks*. The boobies were chiming in with a mixture of *awk* and shrill whistles. As I lay there, I decided I preferred the boobies over the seagulls. The boobies were watching me with thousand-yard stares from their lime-colored eyes. They did not look pleased. It was an interesting scene and situation except for their anger. Looking down, I saw why. Just under my chin was a nest made of dung pushed up and around a white egg.

"Oh," I addressed the birds and scooted back to a safe distance. And stood up. The gulls went nuts with their *gawks* and took flight. So did many of the boobies, but they seemed not as fearful of my presence, such as it was: *a human* with wet, tangled hair, damp, torn-up clothing, and bloodied knees and fingers.

I thought briefly of my grandson, who had once had a fascination with these blue-paint-dipped penguin-ducks. I think I smiled before turning away from them, to the low wall of green foliage and the rest of the island.

I watched my boots carefully work the rocks until the rain stopped falling. I was at the edge of the green jungle. Twenty paces in, the wind was no longer trying to slap me around. Instead of walking straight through, I walked and climbed parallel to the coast as best I could. Not clear why, but it was important at the time. Perhaps to have a bearing in a world turned a million shades of green while I searched for a path, a trail, a four-lane expressway, some hint of which way to go. Everything my hands touched was either slick or sticky. I made my way a hundred yards in before I entered the first swarm of flying insects. The first was low, spiraling flies. Next came the first of many clouds of very hungry and aggressive mosquitos. I had no idea where I was headed, but I needed to pick up the pace before I was eaten alive.

For the next hour, my world was negotiating rocks and tree trunks and slick grasses. Birds squawked up above, and rustling, bounding animals crashed into the vegetation before me. More than a few sounded large enough to take me down while sinking their fangs into my throat.

I came to a clearing of sorts, a patch of gray rocks under an open, green canopy. I stopped for the first time and stood, breathing fast. The air was bitter and sickly sweet. In the sky above, clouds the colors of ash and coal were in chaos. Thunder pounded. The stones under my boots rattled. Ducking low, I kept my eyes raised. The air *cracked*, and lightning exploded in blinding white light. The air went electric, a hot acid smell of ozone. Dropping to the ground, I covered my head as though that would help if a zillion volts struck me.

I stayed prostrate on the rocks for the next five minutes as lightning cracked and blasted. I smelled smoke and burning vegetation mixed with the electric charges. The first strike proved to be the biggest and closest, but with each new one, my body clenched as I cowered.

As abruptly as the lightning and thunder stomped in across the sky overhead, it also crackled and rumbled away fast, like Satan or, worse, some movie-effects lunatic, had called out to me, "Enough yet?"

Dead silence followed. I headed out in roughly the same direction as before, into hanging vines and vibrant green plants and larger rocks to navigate. Ten minutes later, I stopped again to the sound of running and slashing water. Turning from my course for the first time, I followed the sounds to my right.

An eight-foot waterfall was pouring into a basin formed by stones. The pool was roughly twenty-five feet in diameter, the surface calm at my boot toes. I couldn't judge its depth and didn't care. The water was clear and, I assumed, safe. I knelt and drank and drank some more. The water was refreshingly cold and crisp, and I rubbed my face and hands in it before heading off again.

There was a distant sound, a faint mechanical thumping coming from the grass and rocks on the other side of the water. I headed that way.

Back to the climbing and trudging. It seemed I must be somewhat close to the middle of the island. I started up a rock and muck incline and paused, listened, paused again, and heard a similar but different faint vibration in the tangle of green. I climbed to the top of the rise, where the sound was a bit louder. It would buzz for something like two seconds, then pause, then buzz again, over and over. An engine? A generator? I listened to two more series and chose to explore it.

It is a known moviemaking adage to follow the sewer pipe to reach those at the top. I used my boot to press the vegetation aside and saw a gurgling, four-inch, black flex pipe. I began to follow it.

The flex pipe and I walked and climbed, wove and stumbled for ten minutes before a new sound beckoned—this one made me smile. It was the chugging of generators and pumps. At the top of the next rise, I stepped out into the light of the gray, wet sky above and looked across a wide clearing—this one large enough to hold at least half of the stock of Packards back at Gustin's in Detroit.

I stepped past a bulldozer with a grader. The vehicle looked new and abandoned and tired. To my right, the generators and portable pump rumbled and belched out diesel smoke. There were three shipping containers off to my left, and the smashed rock and grass marks from others that had been removed. There was a fuel depot and pallets of disassembled camera trolleys and lighting towers and tool crates. In the center of the clearing, the rocks had been crushed to gravel and graded. A large H for the copters had been formed with white paint. There were tents at the edge of the clearing. I didn't see a single person anywhere.

Another moviemaking fact: if you want to find the set, follow the snaking power cables. I did, along a fine, crushed-gravel road into the trees across the way. I took one look back into the clearing and thought briefly of Seabees, recalling my dead father and his seldom-talked-about military adventures.

The road ran straight for forty yards before a turn. The jungle had been cut above and to the sides to accommodate equipment.

The first person I saw on the island was a teenager in green uniform cradling an automatic weapon, staring into the trees even as my footsteps drew near. I suppose I looked like I fit into the film crew with my wild hair and dirty, casual clothing, because he never looked my way as I passed by, entering the turn to the left. There were two more armed urchins in fatigues between me and the film set. Their leader, commander, whatever, was an adult soldier in black boots, camo pants, and a T-shirt with a studio logo, holding a metal cup and a thermos. I don't know if he was watching me anymore than the kids with guns, because he wore gold-tinted aviator shades. I nodded to him. He drank from his cup.

Walking past him without a word, I made the final turn, and there was the film set. I reverted to my prior mindset and began identifying the premise if not the yet the plot of the film by studying the main building. My impressions and the details percolated.

"Jungle Gothic. Lost love and madness and money long gone."

The primary structure was a three-story narrow home of sorts, suggesting Brooklyn tenement buildings I'd seen in movies, minus the other like structures pressing its sides. It was an uneven and conflicting blend of stone, wood, and bricks used to define a confused façade, surely designed by an unstable mind. Large, wide stairs rose to a worn front door. There were no windows on the first floor, and that level was the worst for wear with flaking paint and uneven clapboards and missing bricks and chipped stones. The second story had a large glass patio door set back from an out-curving stone balcony. The glass had been smashed out and the dirtied lace drapes were hanging out. The third floor was all crumbling brick and had a single window, a small round portal off to the far left. The plants around the building were wildly overgrown and sickly looking, but still living, climbing the structure, which was evenly divided in half by sunlight on the right side and dark and unpleasant green tree shadows on the left. All three floors were painted a once-vibrant gold, but now rot and fading and patches of climbing mold had discolored the structure, turning it to more like faded mustard. I turned away.

Opposite the primary set, crews were at work on other set buildings, deconstructing them. When I was still in high school and working evenings for the Nash Pictures Studio, I'd been part of teams like this, doing the physical side of post-production, the clean-up, the erasing of the evidence of dreams made into celluloid.

There were three guys standing between me and the workers and equipment. One of the men peeled off and walked my way. He didn't look pleased to see me. The other two wore hard hats and tool belts. The guy approaching wore expensive boots, multipocketed shorts, a neutral blue bowling shirt, and I knew he was film crew—he had both a radio on his hip and a cellphone in his hand. He was scowling, and I looked past him to the others. More work crews among tool crates and equipment before half-dismantled sets and structures. I was looking for an executive producer or someone who could bring me up to speed on Pauline.

"Hey," he barked.

Before he reached me, I had him pegged—an assistant producer. That style of voice, its tone, had a singular role in movie production: herding crews to focus on the never-quite-ready next shot.

"Why are you on my set?" His voice cracked the air between us.

I smiled. The use of *my* nailing down his AP role.

"Am I late?" I asked, trying to look lost and confused.

His hostile glare was on my eyes—no, my face. Processing, trying to recall, figure out why I was on *his* film set.

"I'm Pierce Danser," I said, hoping that helped.

Sadly, my name didn't ring a bell. He had a good-looking tan face with the requisite black beard, optional ponytail, and focused gray-blue eyes. I noticed recent nose and jaw work. He was studying my face.

"I'm looking for my wife," I said.

"I've known you." His eyes rose to mine.

I smiled some.

"You were on *Three Knives*. Steadicam famous, right? Ryan Dot's pal, wherever his career is."

"Dot retired from stardom. Who are you?"

"Steven."

"Nice name. *Now*, about my wife?"

His shoulders relaxed and his hands went behind his back.

"Should I care about how you got here? No," he asked and answered himself.

"You're the AP," I said.

"Was. Switched hats now that principal filming is done. I'm now lead location production."

I looked around, and his title decoded. The party was over. Now it was time to clean up the children's mess.

"My wife? *Pauline Place*?" I used her name to rattle him back into focus.

It worked. Sort of. He replied, "Yes…"

"And?" I nudged.

His eyes turned away. I saw bridled anger.

"She wanders off with no word. No hint. Just *poof.* They'll work around it. Got all the money shots. Use back and side shots with her double."

"Wandered off? On this rock of an island? Was she alone?"

He nodded along with questions one and two and stopped at number three.

"Her…minder also disappeared."

"Johal the handsome?"

"There was a flurry of copters," he said, not answering me. "All night long. We know she wasn't on the night launch. I personally called the temporary dock."

"Dock? What dock?" Had I made my jungle *adventure* for naught?

"It's gone. Tore down this morning. That was the first teardown order. The locals…" At that, he looked away to the group of gun-toting adolescents. "And their wildlife reserve or whatever it's called."

"When did the principals leave?" I asked, referring to the *important* players: the director, cast, and the all-mighty producers. Last to land; first to fly off.

"In the night."

"Did they search for—was my wife with them?"

"I don't know."

"Well, you should. *Someone* should."

"It was a clusterfuck here. We were told to wrap midstream. Director got a wild idea, an inspiration, and with Pauline off to who

THE COLLECTORS • 83

knew where, decided the location shoots were done. And believe it or not, we were ahead of schedule."

"I'll never believe that, but okay. So, all these copters come and go, and no one knows if she boarded?"

"Right. Well, no. She had disappeared before. With him."

"The goon? Sorry, Johal?"

"Yes, him. On a private copter. Not one of ours."

I looked out across the location to the workers toiling to erase the sets from the island's memory. I was sweat-soaked and overheated and muscle-tired and, yes, full of doubt. I listened to equipment and voices at work. *What are you doing?* I asked myself. *Chasing all over after someone who left of her own free will?*

The clouds above decided to add to the mood by pouring rain. Steven said something in a kind, non-AP voice.

"What?" I asked.

"Want a lift? We're getting copters tonight."

I didn't answer, bad-mannered me. *Wild goose chase* is what I thought. "No, thank you. I have a ride. I think."

"You do? *And* how did you get here?"

"Friend with a boat."

"And your friend is waiting?"

"You know, that's a good question. I don't know."

"Call him?"

"He's a her and—"

My hand went inside the satchel Walton had packed and rummaged. I felt what must be a plastic bag of rolled tortillas. I felt a bottle of water. And a solid object with nobs and dials.

"My pal Walton," I said to Steven, taking out the radiophone.

CHAPTER NINE

◆ ◆ ◆

TRAWLER

WHEN FILMING was done for the day, the collector oversaw the work crews rolling the twenty-foot panels into place, surrounding the three primary sets for *Dark Liaison*. He had ordered that this happen every night during the production—the difficulty lay in working the temporary walls into place so that they blocked the cameras and lighting equipment. He observed with his back turned, Rolf describing the progress to him among the sounds of wood scraping and mallets smacking and the workers grunting and cursing. After a half hour, the sounds of labor ended, and the footsteps retreated.

"You're good to go, Mr. C," Rolf told the collector.

"You may now call me Deung."

He turned, sweeping the hem of his black silk robe along as he entered the film set used for the previous bathing scene. It was no longer needed, but he had insisted it remain in place. His round, lidless eyes narrowed as his cheeks rose in a smile or grimace of pleasure. He entered the second set, a rebuild of the *Dark Liaison* dank prison cell, his robe gathering and sweeping straw on the stone floor. The cell had stone walls and was about ten-foot square. There was a short wooden bed with a straw mattress—no blankets—a barred window way up high, and a wooden bucket.

Rolf remained at the edge of the second set, looking in, standing side by side with Tacas, who worked for Deung. Tacas was a tall, husky man with a constant blank expression and slow, scanning eyes. Deung crossed the cell to the opposite wall.

"Oh geez," Rolf breathed to Tacas.

Tacas didn't reply or react as Deung swept the skirt of his silk robe and squatted over the wood bucket and voided his bowels.

"I've decided," Deung said to Rolf, pausing to grunt. A hefty *plop* and *splat* were released. "I'm keeping you."

Tacas snapped his fingers and a young girl entered the set with a second wood bucket. She approached the still-squatting Deung hesitantly, her eyes away from his while reaching for the bucket between his knees.

"Not done," his voice gargled.

She froze in place. Her head down, her hands trembling.

Studying Rolf, Deung continued, "We offer full medical, a 401K, a generous pension plan. And a chance for you to stay alive."

Dark liquid splattered and he frowned, as much as his ruined face would allow.

"Guess I'm done," he said sounding sad, and stood, wiping his ass with straw.

The young woman knelt at his side and quickly swapped the buckets. She departed with the used one.

"Follow me," he instructed, and Rolf and Tacas crossed the prison cell as Deung parted the black curtain to the third set.

It was the scene of the movie's ending: the Gothic church, the forced wedding. Hundreds of candles lit the altar and decorations of adornment on the stone walls. The altar was constructed of old and dark worn boards.

"Shame we don't have the time to film this final scene," Deung said. "She was amazing, startling, in the original."

His scarred hand shook and glided along the rail before the first pew.

"Here I am in full makeup, and she's being difficult. I understand that's common in her profession. That will change."

Deung looked to his hand and his chest. The makeup somewhat masked the scars and ruined skin. His face was also made up in an unsuccessful effort to plaster and paint his disfigured features.

"Mr. C, my apologies," Tacas nudged demurely, "the schedule."

"Yes," Deung agreed, still looking at Rolf. "Is *she* ready? Willing?"

"She's ready," Rolf answered. "Willing? Well, the meds are working their wonders."

"See to having *my* precious Pauline taken to the copter."

"It's already happening," Rolf replied, looking away from the ruined face of Deung in his open silk robe.

"And your former boss, the butterball?" Deung asked. "And Mr. Rand and the ship's crew?"

"They all ate the same dessert," Tacas spoke up. "Same with the film crew."

The veins on Deung's face reddened with pleasure. Rolf looked away.

"I'll have this set rebuilt at home," Deung said, taking one last look before starting back through the prior sets with Tacas and Rolf in tow.

Back out on the soundstage, three of Deung's employees approached. They wore work packs and carried canvas tool bags.

"Everything in place?" Tacas asked them, speaking on Deung's behalf.

"Port and starboard stabilizers are primed," the tallest worker said.

"I want to do it," Deung chimed, his voice delighted.

"Let's get topside first, sir," Tacas suggested.

"Mr. C, sir, do you really need to do this?" Rolf braved, looking at the three workers.

"Yes and *shut it*—don't speak again unless I ask you to. I want this offshore studio *retired* without a trace to me."

Small feet pattered on the steel floor, and Deung looked into the shadows beyond his employees.

"Oh, my ducklings," he said to the two young girls who had previously been employed by Mr. Rand. The girl on the left held clothing in her arms.

"We won't be needing that," he said to the one with the bucket. "Dress me."

Both girls were wild-eyed and trembling with fright.

"Calm yourselves," Deung commanded. "You're the lucky two—you get to come home with me."

The girl to the left stutter-walked closer with the clothing. She opened the waistband of a pair of black silk pants and he stepped into them. That done, he shrugged off his robe and let it fall. The girl's head lowered and turned away. Deung was getting an erection just a few inches from her face.

"Oh no!" Rolf let out, caught herself, and added quickly, "My apologies."

The girl held up the black silk shirt, and Deung took it in his scarred hands and pulled it over his mostly bald head.

He stepped forward, banging against the girl intentionally and toppling her. He and the rest of entourage walked to the door from the soundstage for the last time. The group stepped out into the narrow hall and walked to the traversing metal stairs.

Up top, Deung led the way in through the door to the bridge, which was unmanned. Two of his employees bustled to the helm to look over the controls as the other accelerated the autopilot. Deung stepped to the view of the helipad where his helicopter was warming up. Two of his employees were assisting his co-star Pauline Place into the chopper. She was placid, and her shoe tips dragged until she was hefted up inside.

"Call the punk with the stupid glasses," he said to Tacas. "Confirm that some of her personal belongings are being sent over. Want her to be cozy."

Tacas took his radiophone off his belt.

Deung turned around to the two frightened girls. "Get on board."

The two looked to one another, spoke, and scampered out the glass door and across the dark ship deck to the helicopter. Tacas opened his tool bag and offered Deung the two remotes. Deung took one in each hand and placed his thumbs on the orange fire buttons.

"I like this part." Deung sounded pleased, delighted. He pressed the button in his left hand and the one in the right.

The muffled explosion was felt more than heard, then followed by a second blast. The helm windshield and the slide glass door rattled, and the bridge shook from both sides and underneath.

"Rumble to the left, rumble to the right," Deung singsonged childishly.

His three employees dropped their work packs and tool bags and went out into the night. Tacas caught the door before it shut and held it open for his employer.

Deung stood still, looking at the helm for the last time. Alarms were going off and displays were blinking red alerts.

"She'll flounder fast," Tacas said.

"I know that. I'm trying for *last regards* to Fatima et al. Can't find it in my heart. Let's go."

Three minutes later, Deung and his employees were seated and belted into their seats. The propeller above cycled up into a furious spin as the engines revved harsh and loud. The helicopter rose and swiveled fifty feet above and off to the side of the trawler. Deung pressed his forehead against his window. He noted the sabotaged and sinking lifeboats and saw the first of five small but bright explosions inside the bridge. Air and water were boiling at the trawler's hips, which were already waddling lower in the sea.

He put on the headset and spoke to Tacas. "What do you think? An hour?"

"Less, sir. I'd say fifteen minutes. The charges were a bit stronger than planned."

"That will work. Get me home. There is still a lot of work to do tonight."

Deung watched the sinking trawler until the helicopter nose dipped, and they accelerated away.

CHAPTER TEN

◆ ◆ ◆

MOMENTUM

IN THE last of the day's light, I started my sweaty, insect-eaten tromp back to the sea, to that kitten-tongue cove. Halfway across that foul and scary island, I stopped and took out the radiophone. In the remaining light, I looked over the device, with its many buttons and dials. I pushed and twisted all of them and spoke into the mouthpiece, never getting a reply.

Maybe I should have waited for the night copter, but waiting around hadn't seemed right. That said, my momentum-instead-of-planning was feeling less than best.

I ate a tortilla and continued at a quicker pace because of the failing light, which meant that I tripped and fell more often as the air filled with clouds of mosquitos.

I was fortunate. My first trip across this rock had been so clumsy that I had cut a pretty wide swath and broke and trampled the vegetation. When there was muck, I retraced my boot prints. When I had no clue, I tried to go forward in a straight line.

When I came out of the jungle, there was enough light to avoid stepping into booby nests. I walked gingerly across the gray rocks and grass, greeted by gulls and boobies. All squawking and *awking* and whistling. Approaching the cliff, I kept my eyes to my boots for two reasons: not to step on birds or eggs, and to delay the likely disappointment of seeing the ocean barren of the *Viewfinder*.

It wasn't there. I sat down on a rock, head in hands.

Doubts about my decisions and actions; my attempt to rescue my wife. Too much self-propulsion instead of clever planning, or just plain old planning.

I looked up.

All the questioning and regrets dissolved into pixie dust.

Running lights shone past the southern rocks, and the radio crackled. I took it out and pushed the talk button.

"Thank you," I said, stowed the radiophone inside my satchel, and climbed over the ledge. My descent was graceless and painful in the dark all the way down. I found a slippery footing on a rock that disappeared with each swell. From water level, I couldn't see the *Viewfinder*. A spotlight swept the rocks to my left. Waiting long enough to believe it would stay constant, I dove into the ocean.

As I swam out of the cove, wishing I had removed my boots, I was glad I was in pretty good shape. I swam along the path laid by that great white light, rising and falling in the aggressive swells.

Climbing the transom ladder was a struggle. I had exhausted the last of my strength. Up on deck, I bent over and panted and took a minute before looking up.

"Thank you," I got out.

Walton handed me a folded towel.

"Get dry fast," she said over her shoulder. "We've got a problem."

"We do?" I followed her inside, to the lower helm.

"Well, not us, but—I'll explain." She gathered up a log book and turned to me. "Join me at the top helm."

Up top, Walton went to the wheel, her lovely face and focused eyes lit by the glow of various, colored displays.

She handed me the binoculars. "Take a seat."

I did and held the field glasses in my lap.

She brought the *Viewfinder* quickly up to speed. Over the next five minutes, she made three radio calls and got no response. I watched her place one of her small fingers on a blip on one of the displays, press it, and keep it there. I continued holding the binoculars in my hands, wanting to ask what was up, but also not wanting to disturb her focus and efforts. Her body and arms were tense, and she had yet to look my way.

Five minutes away from Black Island, the *Viewfinder* ran in the night, a pair of running lights skimming across the black water.

"You should get something to eat," she said, finally breaking her silence.

I did, finding an apple and two tortillas in her ice chest. I passed on the pale, gooey cheese stuff. Sitting back beside Walton, I took a bite of apple and her hand went out. I handed her the apple, and she quickly consumed half of it.

"Tortilla?" I offered, my voice warbling in the wind.

We exchanged the half apple for a rolled tortilla.

While still working the radio, she turned.

"There's a distress signal. Someone's having a very bad night."

I looked out through the windshield. All I could see was black sea under the black sky.

We traveled without talking for forty minutes. Heading west, out to sea and away from shore. I confirmed that by the compass numbers in light blue font on one of the displays. I looked to her delicate finger still pressed on the orange blip on the center display. We were closing in on it.

Five minutes later, Walton brought the throttles up fast and we slowed aggressively. Her hand went into my lap and took up the field glasses. She raised hers and I found a second pair, long forgotten, in the store box under the dash. I raised them and looked in the same direction as Walton. Then I lowered them. They weren't needed. We were about a hundred yards away.

The tip of the ship's bow was vertical in the black sea. Water was boiling, filled with clutter. Large metal groans were somehow reaching us from below the surface.

We watched the nose of the ship continue its final descent.

"Scan for survivors," Walton said softly.

We waited and scanned and watched the trawler sink. Walton steered the *Viewfinder* in a circle around the rising fountain of released air among what had escaped and still floated.

"No survivors," she radioed ten minutes later. She spoke with the mic under her binoculars. We were both still scanning the surface.

"No name on the boat," she said a minute later.

The radio spoke: "Was being tracked. In fact, it had been on screen, but refusing all calls, all attempts at ID. No calls for assistance. We need you to pull back one kilometer."

Walton turned our boat, and we retreated as requested.

The Coast Guard helicopter arrived first. Then one of their small, fast boats. By that time, we had been looking for survivors among the debris for twenty minutes. As the copter lights swept and searched, there was very little for them to see. The trawler and its crew were erased, swallowed by the sea.

We were asked to step back further, so to speak, when a larger Coast Guard cutter entered the scene. Walton obliged, quickly turning the *Viewfinder* away from the spot where the trawler had sunk.

"Nothing to see up here," Walton said. "I'm going down to the lower helm."

I remained on the flying bridge. I had an uneasy feeling as we turned away. More than tragedy, I felt a personal sadness that I didn't understand, but accepted.

Walton and I sailed back across the sea, and a couple of hours later she turned the *Viewfinder* into the familiar, rock-lined harbor. The village looked dead or asleep or both. A single street light before a cannery was the only illumination.

She and I moored the *Viewfinder*, working together; she dropped the forward anchor, and I fumble-released the stern one. We met back up at the port rail, where I took off my boots and draped them around my neck.

"I'd take you across in the dinghy, but…" She smiled, faint and brief.

"Thank you. For everything."

Her steady, beautiful eyes were tired. I opened my arms for a hug, and her smile tilted as her hands pressed my shoulders, keeping me back.

"You're welcome. Now go find your wife."

I shouldered my satchel and climbed the rail. I was beside the Willy some ten minutes after diving into the foul harbor water. Wonder of wonders, the Jeep wasn't up on rocks or blocks and still had four tires.

A portly child, perhaps seven years old, in ragtag clothing stepped over as I climbed in. He pressed my shoulder with his chubby fist.

"*Guardado el Jeep*," he said, and I watched his fist open in expectation.

An elderly woman had the boy's back, three steps away.

"*Dinero*," the boy demanded. This was a child with mean-dog eyes.

I dug through my satchel and found my soggy wallet at the bottom.

I offered him a twenty.

His head shook and the woman took a step closer. I slid out two more dank twenties and that did the trick. He took the bills and turned to her. While they conversed, I started the Willy, found reverse, and backed away from them, not quite spinning the tires.

The next hour was nothing except the headlights illuminating cobblestone, then dirt roads and errant sections of pavement with the jungle sliding past me on both sides. The roads were empty except for a few big old trucks that preferred the center line, which, in all fairness, rarely appeared. I got lost a few times, not saying how many times, before I parked in front of the dark villa.

No oil lantern, no Señor Brisca greeted me. I crossed the first two dark and overgrown rooms and climbed the stairs to the tall rolling door and the brightly lit living area. The great room appeared empty at first, flavored with the dazzling scents of beef and sauces cooking. My nose led my eyes. No one was at the large stove. I spotted the two women I had seen in the kitchen before, their heads barely visible before one of the centered couches. One of the women, the stout one, stood, facing me. I took one last breath of wonderful cooking aromas and walked to them.

Sara lay on the couch before them. One of the women held a towel of ice to the side of her head. The other woman tracked me with sharp eyes, and I saw the seriously long butcher knife gripped in her hand, held ready to plunge into my chest.

I stepped back and pasted on a smile of sorts. The knife remained poised. I looked down to Sara.

My guess was that she had been struck twice. A vicious blow to the side of the head had left a gash on her temple and blood in the wound in her tangled hair. She had also been hit in the jaw and mouth. The lower part of her face was cut and swollen, and her nose and lips were bloodied. Her left eye was purple and puffed closed. She was awake, but didn't look aware or present. Her good eye was vacantly aimed to the kneeling woman.

Mindful of that long, sharp knife, I slowly, slowly extended my hand over the arm of the couch and lightly brushed the top of Sara's hair.

Sara's hand rose and gripped mine.

The two women spoke to one another in Spanish.

"Señor Brisca?" I asked.

They appeared to not hear.

"Señor Ethan?" I tried.

The knife rose.

Not a good topic.

The woman holding the ice towel to Sara's head spoke without looking up. "Your *compadre* Ethan did this."

I was surprised and grateful she spoke English. I was also furious. The travel buddy I had brought to the villa had attacked Sara, in Pauline's home.

Sara's confused eye was tracing the conversation, but she still hadn't spoken.

"How are you?" I said to her. "I'm so sorry." I leaned closer.

Her gaze didn't change.

"Where is he?" I asked the kneeling woman.

"Your Ethan left with the truck," she answered.

I scanned the areas of the vast room. "And Señor Brisca?"

The woman with the knife turned and spat on the tile.

"He drove the truck," the kneeling woman said.

"Pierce?" Sara whispered, her voice passive and uncertain.

"I'm here, Sara."

Her good eye closed.

"Have you called the police?" I asked.

The stout woman sent off a second spit.

"Will she be okay?" I asked the woman with the ice cloth.

"Yes, I think so. I radioed for the doctor."

I looked about the great room again. Not only were all the ashtrays gone, but books had been removed, leaving the library shelves looking gap-toothed.

"What else was taken?"

"I'll show you." The kneeling woman stood. She was short and thin and had a frightened, determined expression.

"What is your name?" I asked gently.

"Titi, please."

"Okay, Titi, show me."

The woman with the knife stepped up to the couch and aimed her glaring eyes at the rolling door. Her free hand extended out over Sara.

"Good idea," I told her and followed Titi through that same door, closing it fully.

Upstairs, Pauline's front room looked much the same, except the flowers and ashtrays were gone. We entered Pauline's bedroom where her closet doors and dresser drawers were opened and mostly cleaned out.

Titi and I stood at the back of the couch facing the bed. Her hand went out and lifted the blue and gold necktie draping the leather.

"Mr. Johal. A disgusting man," she said.

"Why do you say that?"

"He sleeps in here when she is gone. Like a king."

She bunched the tie and pushed it into her apron pocket.

I had to ask. "Does he sleep in here when she is home?"

"He wishes," she said. "I see how he watches her."

A heaviness lifted from inside my chest. I looked at the bed. The unshared bed. And I realized I was thinking of the wrong worry.

"The truck?" I asked.

"Yes?"

"Do you know where it took everything?"

"Mr. Danser, no."

"Let's go." I turned from the room.

Back in the living room, I didn't see the guard with her knife at first, then spotted her to my right, standing sentry over Sara, who sat in the monitor glow of her desk. She was holding the ice cloth with one hand and typing with the other. I climbed onto the raised floor and stood behind her. I offered the big, well-armed woman my finest smile. I gently kissed the top of Sara's head.

"Whatcha up to, no? Are you okay?" I asked her.

"My vision is a bit fucked up, but I'm good."

"What happened?"

"Better ask Titi. Ethan knocked me out. From behind—that worm."

"Then he robbed the place?"

"Seems so. One second."

A light was blinking on her radiophone console. Sara reached across with her free hand and connected the call.

"Hello, Sara. We've located the producer, and if you'll hold just a moment longer, I'll transfer you."

Before Sara could say a word, the call was put on hold.

"Bozo," she said to the polite, professional woman who was no longer on the call. "Can't find Pauline," Sara said to me. "Johal the pig is missing too. Well, not taking calls. Probably ran off."

She turned to her large monitor and continued typing an email flagged urgent to a name I didn't know, but suspected was with the studio.

"I'm gonna go look," I said and decided at the same time. I stepped past the woman with a knife.

"Pierce? What? Look for what?" Sara's voice was regaining a bit more strength.

Before I opened the rolling door, I replied, "The truck."

◆ ◆ ◆

ME AND my momentum issue. I drove those narrow jungle roads for a couple of hours, scanning and driving way too fast, but that was okay; I never saw another vehicle. I drove north first, all the way to the airport, which was a bust. The only lights were from the four parking-lot lamps. The airport was middle-of-the-night dead. Not a single interior light. There were trucks, lots of them, and that was the problem. I had no idea what *my* truck looked like.

I drove south, past the turnoff into the villa road, the Willy straining to stay in stride with my braking, accelerating, and steering. Miles of flickering green walls and nothing more in the headlight beams. The last section of pavement ended, and the tires raised dust, moving at a good enough pace so I didn't have to breathe it. The road snaked and climbed into the hills. I rounded turn after turn. Mile after mile. And was brake-tested by a cattle gate.

I stopped short of crashing into it. I was tired and frustrated and, by stopping, I realized two things: the Willy was near empty of gasoline, and I had no idea what the hell I was doing. Me and my momentum, indeed. I tucked in my tail, turned the Willy around, and returned to Pauline's villa.

◆ ◆ ◆

SARA WAS awake and resting on the couch in the care of Titi and protected by the brave knife wielder. She gave me a wan smile and closed her eyes.

"The studio doesn't know anything," she whispered. "If it helps, they're pissing all over themselves and planning a search with the locals. I bet half their staff is cooking up denials."

I looked from Sara to the pool yard. The sky was early-morning blue. Sunrise would be soon.

"You rest," I told Sara.

There was a spare blanket on the arm of the couch at her feet. I gathered it up and went out into the chill air. I sat down on the nearest lounge. I planned to lay down, cover myself, and accept the pull to sleep I was feeling deep in my body and my sinking mind. I laid down, resting my head on my arm. My eyes stung with exhaustion. My worries were holding their ground as I pulled the blanket over my head in response. Daylight would provide clarity and resources, the likely well-greased police, and even the media, if need be.

Insects were clicking in the surrounding hedges and small birds were waking and chirping, and the air was fresh, unlike what it would become when the hot sun rose. Sleep momentum was erasing my rescue momentum, and I closed my eyes.

Two deep breaths later, they reopened. Moving without a thought, I got up, went inside, and sat at Sara's desk.

I recall saying, "Phone." I had a few telephone numbers still stored in my memory. I dialed Rhonda.

CHAPTER ELEVEN

◆ ◆ ◆

THE COLLECTOR

DEUNG'S HELICOPTER landed on the northern helipad, which was closer to his villa than the southern one used by his employees. He stepped down first and stood on his football-field-sized rolling lawn, eyeing his favorite residence; his palazzo, his version of the Villa Capra "La Rotonda" in Vicenza, Italy. The immense lawn was mowed low twice a week. For his gardeners, the real battle was with the jungle trying to take palazzo hostage, climbing the sides and obscuring, consuming, the six-story white-stone walls. So far, his ground crew were defeating the attack.

Rolf and Tacas joined him, standing one stride back. Two employees lowered Pauline from the copter and eased her into a wheelchair. Mr. Rand's two girls stepped down and joined the employees, as instructed midflight, rolling the famous actress across the lawn to the west side of the compound. The helicopter prop slowed to a stop and the swirling wind settled.

Deung stood still, waiting, looking to the great stairs leading to the building-length portico. His house staff appeared as one, all thirty employees lining up between the immense six columns. He spent a full minute reviewing his house and staff before raising his right hand, signaling his approval. The row of employees began to applaud as he started across the lawn to them.

He was sweating by the time he reached the steps, his makeup melting and forming slow rivers on his skin. He climbed with some effort, Rolf and Tacas at his back to each side. He paused at the top of the stairs as he entered the shade of the portico, where all the members of his staff took steps back, forming a V for him to enter. Deung started along the three-story-high corridor with its many ornate frescos, all featuring images of *statues*; most of them famous, others personal. He gazed side to side, walking leisurely with Rolf and Tacas and his staff in tow. The frescos featured a mix of historical characters and film stars of the past fifty decades. At the end of the corridor, he entered the circular-domed rotunda with its high, ornamental ceiling. Crossing the substantial room, he raised his right hand again, and in response, his staff winged off to the doorways to his sides and behind. At the far end of the room, there were double doors with a finely detailed pediment above. Two women in white dinner jackets and no other clothing stood at attention. They opened both two-story doors as he drew close. He stepped through, still trailed by Rolf and Tacas, and took ten strides and paused until the doors were closed behind.

All vestige of the beautifully recreated Villa Capra was gone. The three stood in another building, another era—the current one. They were in a three-story atrium of steel and two-story windows. The ceiling was retracted, and the air was fresh and cooled by silent air conditioners. On each side were three detached modern apartments.

"Pick a suite, Rolf," Deung said, not turning around.

She walked off to the left, not saying a word.

Tacas followed Deung to the middle of the courtyard before he also angled away to the right, to his suite. Deung continued on solo, making his way to the glass door in the opposing glass and steel wall. He opened the door and stepped into sunlight shrouded by the limbs of a mature olive grove. There was a narrow path of crushed peach coral that led into the grove, and he walked it until reaching his personal residence, some fifty yards up through the trees.

His residence was an unadorned, unattractive warehouse-looking building. He unlocked the steel door by placing his scarred palm on the security pad and stepped into the air-conditioned office foyer with its weak purple carpeting, the shade of dusty lilac. The walls were imported teak from Selangor, Malaysia, and there was no furniture, just three fine doors at the opposite end of the room.

Deung took a black parka off the hook beside the front door and pulled it on. The sterilized air was climate controlled to a crisp fifteen degrees Celsius.

His mum and father were there to greet him, facing the room not as a couple, but from both side walls. Both were smiling, their eyes and expressions were set to delight. Deung looked to his mum first—her eternal smile kind and caring to him. She was formally dressed in an elegant, commanding, olivine Nina McLemore design. Her ornate necklace, rings, and earrings featured the pink-clear diamonds that were the illicit source of his parent's wealth, now all his. Deung nodded his approval to her, liking her latest pose in the glass case where a gentle chemical breeze was lightly ruffling her dress hem.

"Welcome home, Mr. Deung," Allister John, his curator and assistant, spoke from the center of the room.

Deung ignored him and looked across to his father, who wore tux and tails and a well-preserved bullet hole in the center of his forehead. His expression was forced to pleasantness, and his glass eyes shone at his son. Deung widened his cheeks and revealed all his teeth to his father.

Allister stood patiently with a thick folio open in his hands. He wore an immaculate Brooks business suit, and his silver hair had recently been buzz cut. Deung turned to him and reached for the folio as he started across to the three doors. He carried the folio through the middle door with Allister in tow. The two took the opposing chairs at Deung's long, wide, teak desk. Deung poured himself a glass of ice water and slid the pitcher across. He opened the folio while Allister poured himself some water.

The folio was half tablet computer, the other side offering a number of spreadsheets. Deung took up a red pen and read with it, ignoring the glowing tablet to the left. There was a series of tasks along the left-hand column with associated status and note fields. He scanned all five pages quickly, then returned to the first page and began again slowly.

"Revenues up seventeen percent. Keep making me happy."

He removed his parka. The office was a tepid twenty-four degrees Celsius. Allister took a sip of water.

"Ensure Ms. Place is cozy," Deung said. "She's being temperamental when not medicated. And get our hands back on her sons, for now."

"As you ask, yes."

Deung looked up from the folio. Allister was looking past him out the window. A glint of sunlight had sparked off the corner of the hangar-sized studio back in the jungle.

"Am I boring you?" Deung said.

"Not at all. My apologies."

"Accepted. How are things in the surgery? Never mind, I'll go look in a few minutes."

"Yes. As you can see," Allister said, gazing at the folio in Deung's hands, "all is on track. I hope you'll be pleased."

"I see that the Rosalia cadaver arrived."

"Yes. It's not in the notes, but her modified display is nearly complete."

"You're dismissed." Deung spoke to his hands.

Allister stood, picked up Deung's parka from the floor, and carried it from the office.

Deung turned his attention to the tablet in the folio, tapping it to life. He worked in email for an hour, communicating with his blood diamond partners for twenty minutes. He spent a half hour reaching out to suppliers of cast members and film producers. Swiveling his chair, he looked out to the rounded, sheet-metal roof of his studio, off in the trees.

"Deung is conflicted," he said to himself looking to the view before standing and leaving his office. "*He* thinks again that the movies just are not enough."

Out in the foyer, he entered the door to the right of his office and entered the surgery.

The light was clinically bright and the worktables and equipment were steel and aluminum. The surgery was divided into four areas, each with a different floor color that segregated the teams and technologies. He entered the green area, where a team of two females were hard at work at taxidermy restoration. Their specimens were mounted and posed and being gently cared for and treated. Deung raised a finger, as though to ask a question, but he didn't speak, not wanting to disturb their focus.

He entered the yellow area where freeze-dry equipment and containers were being operated and maintained. The specimens the yellow team was working with were inside the containers. Deung stepped past to the viewing window, not bothering to gaze inside; there hadn't been any changes or additions to the specimens.

He walked along the back wall filled by rows of square aluminum doors, stopping in front of each to examine its hanging ID tag.

Allister joined him, one stride back, and addressed Deung's unspoken question.

"Yes, we're full."

Deung didn't respond, and Allister fell into stride with his boss as he stepped away.

"We're nearly overrun by incoming shipments," Allister explained.

Deung gave him a pensive nod.

The two men entered the blue area, the largest, due to the size and complexity of the equipment. This was the latest, most high-tech area, where plastination—the latest preserving technology—was worked. The technicians were busy at the computer consoles before the walk-in plastination units, working to a smooth electronic hum.

"New equipment?" Deung asked, pointing his disfigured hand to the partially unpacked shipping crates.

"Yes, sir, they're behind schedule. As you saw in the notes, blue team needs additional headcount."

"Approved."

"Good, sir. I've selected three candidates at the von Hagen lab. I'll get them hired and sent over."

"From Heidelberg?"

"No, sir, the Kyrgyzstan Institute. Staff there are easier to *persuade.*"

Deung walked to the black area, which was the smallest and staffed by two female technicians or "caregivers," as he preferred to call them. There were three specimens being cared for, each in its own hermetically sealed glass case.

"There's my little girl," Deung said warmly, kneeling before the latest arrival, nudging a technician aside. The woman slid away from him from where she had been working on swapping out the old life-support equipment with the latest chemical induction unit.

Deung knelt, resting his hand on the glass, and kindly brushed it as he gazed down on the sleeping, beautiful, fairly well-preserved face of Rosalia Lombardo, who had died nearly a hundred years before. Her father, distraught over her loss of life, had had his little girl embalmed by Salafia in Palermo.

Acquiring Rosalia had been a protracted and expensive effort, finally accomplished by Allister under the guise of a loan to a nonexistent but well-documented museum.

"She is adorable," Allister offered softly from behind Deung.

"It is true," Deung agreed.

The little girl had wheat-colored curls of hair. There was a single yellow bow on the crown of her head. Her age-discolored garment was lovingly nestled under her chin and over her slight shoulders and body. The face of the angelic child had a tan skin tone, not from sunlight, but from the archaic embalming technology available at the turn of the previous century.

"Will the new equipment improve her skin tone?" Deung asked the technician at his side.

"No, sir, not yet, but give us another nine months."

"Done."

Allister made a note on his computer tablet.

"You will be a delightful addition to the collection," Deung said to the small child. "We'll make you your own centerpiece."

Allister made another note.

"I want a realistic tableau designed. Her father's home, the room where she took her last *living* breath, not the Capuchin catacombs they abandoned her in."

"Yes, sir, I thought you might want such. Research and design has already been started."

"I want a diorama large enough for me to enter. Not a display to look into. A place I can wander. Experience."

"We could reconstruct the entire residence."

Deung paused to consider, his hand still softly brushing the glass case.

"No," he said. "Just the death scene."

Allister typed instead of speaking.

Deung rose to his feet slowly, his eyes never leaving the charming, calm, peaceful face of Rosalia.

"You are my lovely," he said to the ninety-year-old little girl.

Allister followed Deung back through the surgery to the door to the foyer, which Deung entered alone. He nodded to his mum across the faint purple carpet before opening the third door, to the left of his office.

CHAPTER TWELVE

• • •

CABALLEROS

IN MY previous life before restoring Packards for Howie Gustin, my passions were cinematography and Pauline. Truth be told, she had two-thirds. Our marriage was the plum in the fruit salad of popular moviemaking. And honestly, it was a lot of fun. More importantly, my wife and I were believers in the philosophy of the once-famous actor Ryan Dot, who said it best, "Be good. And interested."

Pauline's and my scheduling conflicts were a delight for many years, making our reunions all the more passionate and happy. As our stars ascended in our different crafts, our schedules became an issue because we lost control of them. Success bred added layers of management and worse; we both allowed studio whims and madness grab our steering wheels.

When Pauline and I argued, it was witty and fun. We never fought. When we were together, we did what the best of lovers do: we danced eye to eye in each other's embrace.

Seven years ago, there was a financial irregularity in Pauline's books. Scratch that—wheelbarrows of cash were rolled from her royalties and escrow and points accounts. Pauline brought in a hired gun, a third-party accounting lawyer. The lawyer went through the

books and traced the irregularities back to the studio. Pauline offered to share the scandal with the authorities and, worse, the press.
The studio, now defunct, took to smiling and offering restitution
and reconciliation—with their eyes on the *dull* edge of the guillotine
blade poised high up above.

One of Pauline's most effective gunslingers was Rhonda.

Pauline and I admired Rhonda's effective navigating of the studio piranha pool; most importantly, we developed a trust in her. In
the following years, we kept Rhonda obscenely overpaid and had her
seated just outside whichever studio Pauline was working for. She
became our knife blade, if you will; hip deep in the industry swamp.
She applied her sharp intelligence and keen taste for blood in the water. Over time, Pauline and I developed a fond and caring friendship
with her. Part of her role was schedule negotiation and being our
communications pipeline. And, the rarest of all, she was our confi-
dant. Even more so when our marriage began to falter.

My decision to walk away from the cameras had Pauline's bless-
ings and loving encouragement. "One of us should get grounded in
that far real world," she told me many times.

And why did I walk? At first it was a lark; trailing my good
friend Ryan Dot who, unlike me, had many detailed and well-
thought-through reasons for no longer wanting to be a featured face
in the dream machine. He liked machines and became a devotee to
those that did more than construct celluloid emotions.

The fault was mine. I grew enamored with the Packards. Place
part A and bolt it to part B and *voila*, metal-on-metal transporta-
tion. A year passed. Dot's work was admired, and I was threatened
but never fired. Both Pauline and I lived in our separate, happy bub-
bles, with airplanes our means for adjoining. The division in our
marriage appeared at the end of that first year, when I flew to her
after Rhonda scheduled a midsummer reunion during a break in
primary filming.

What happened? My mouth. My inability to tie down my
tongue that *needed* to wag in front of her peers and the favored and

pretentious and even the truly good and gifted. When my cameras and I were industry insiders, my caustic wit and unrestrained observations had been tolerated and, honestly, enjoyed and encouraged. Not so when I appeared on locations or on sets in my raggedy work clothes with my yapping mouth.

While I was still admired for my *previous* film craft, it was clear that I was being treated like an annoying motormouth and, worse, passé.

I embarrassed my darling Pauline. More times than I'm *not* brave enough to count. There was the start of our stilted goodbyes when I flew back to Detroit and Packards; later, there was my glee in turning away from that world, that bubble, in favor of scrap searches for non-rust-pitted automobile parts.

Our remaining bond was our two boys, our young men in their good and interested, real-world lives. We discussed them all the more; our telephone conversations were confined to that neutral area, that wonderful topic.

The fissure widened with last year's Oscars. Pauline was again attending, not as a recipient, but as a loved and admired member of that world. Quite simply, she asked me not to join her. No explanation needed—we both experienced the realization that came with no explanation being given. I received the legal separation documents at Gustin's a few weeks later.

So that's where we were. We had our sons and our shared conduit and resource: Rhonda, whose telephone was on its seventh ring.

Rhonda picked up at the start of the eighth ring. Her voice sounded wet, and water was running in the background.

"Wha?" she gurgled.

"Can we trace a radiophone?" I asked.

"*We?* No, but I think I can. Hi Pie. Do you know what kind?"

I described what Ethan's radiophone looked like.

"I think that's a satellite phone. To answer your question, yes. That's an old model. The new Iridiums are neat-o."

"Neat-o?"

"Sorry. Dating a wealthy executive. Did I mention wealthy? Has a great mind, but is stuck in the sixties."

"Rhonda."

"Yes. Focusing. Has he or she called you from it?"

I paused to consider, closing my eyes. The background water sound helped my memory some. Also made me want to pee.

"Yes, he said he had called me in Detroit."

"Okay, good. We'll start with that traffic. I'll need a while."

"How long is a while? Never mind, do your best."

The waterfall tempo changed as though interrupted. Rhonda let out a laugh, just shy of a giggle.

"My wealthy exec just got out of the pool. Ever viewed an elderly naked body that hasn't been exposed to sunlight for more than a few decades?"

"Actually no, I haven't. I did see Caesar Romain in his casket. Lovely service."

"Close, Pie. Now visualize Caesar *sans apparel*."

"Do I have to?"

"Only if you want to laugh with me. Oh geez, he's walking over to me. One sec."

The tempo of the water changed again.

"Where are you?" I asked.

"Poolside shower. Just changed the temp to cold."

I had to laugh. Rhonda joined me.

"Oh goody, he's taking a lounge."

"Goody?"

She didn't explain this season's retro-minded boyfriend. Instead, she said, "Pauline had me hire bodyguards for Bill and Tim."

That brought the levity to an end. Nothing like hearing my sons' names mentioned in that context. I felt a chill, like cold water clearing my mind and gripping my heart.

"This is related to Pauline's disappearances?" I asked slowly.

"Must be, and Pierce? The monies she had me transfer to the still-untraced holding company have been returned."

"What does that say to you?"

"Pie, she's stopped talking to me."

That stopped me quick. More chilled water.

"I'm researching," Rhonda continued. "I'll find the name hiding inside the untraced company, but that's now a lower priority."

"What does this say to you?" I repeated.

"Leverage, Pie. There's only one with her."

"The boys."

"Yes."

"Were they threatened?"

"Only Pauline can say. My vote is yes. Explains the secreted monies. A payoff."

"Then the money is returned? Help me understand."

"One. Pauline has disappeared a second time. Two. Whatever the extortionist wants has changed. He might well now have his ransom. His prize."

"My wife."

"Yes, dear. Now excuse me, time to end playdate here and get to work. Where are you? Still with Sara by chance?"

"Yes."

"Okay, I'll send you trace info. Map it, if I can. Pierce?"

"Yes?"

"Know how to print off a computer?"

"Well…"

"Have Sara help you. And Pie? It'll sound corny, but find her. No, rescue her."

"Yes." We ended the call.

Forty-five minutes later, Titi came to the desk with Sara's phone in her hand. She offered to me, saying, "Miss Sara says you have a message. You print it, she said."

I looked into the big room. Sara was resting, lying low before the maid with the long knife standing before her. What might take a propeller-head a few clicks took me twenty-five minutes, but it resulted in Sara's printer warming from the dead and spitting out a half page of meaningless coordinates.

"Gotta love Rhonda," I said to the warm piece of paper. She had used a pen to draw an invaluable idiot-proof map.

◆ ◆ ◆

I SAT with Sara until the village doctor had blessed her condition and given her a healing prognosis. Titi took my satchel and returned it weighed down.

"Water and food," she told me.

"Any of that cheese?" mouthy me had to ask.

She smiled and said no more, turning her worried and caring attention to Sara.

I squeezed Sara's hand, kissed the uninjured side of her head, and left.

After crossing through those two cavernous front rooms, I stood out in the hot sunlight, map in hand, staring at the Willy. It was a clear choice over the remaining Mercedes coupe, except for one issue—the Willy had a near-empty gas tank. I located the garage set back a ways from the coupe, and inside found two five-gallon cans of gasoline.

I was out on the narrow, dangerous roads in no time, me and my trusty Willy, skinny tires and all.

Ever try and align a childish, if accurately drawn, road map to suspect roads through a jungle in a foreign country? You should try it. Better ye than me.

Nothing looked familiar to me from my previous travels. Every twist and turn and, I admit, reverse and turn were new to me. I worried about getting completely off track, I worried about running out of fuel, I worried the most about having to stop for directions and be consumed by insects and cruel birds and carnivores that slithered and had rows of teeth. I carried on, the threatening jungle flicking alongside the Willy as I steered one bad road after another.

Then something did look familiar. With the Willy locked up and skidding in the dirt and dust, there was that cattle gate I had nearly crashed into the night before.

I spread the map out on my thigh and looked back and forth from it to the metal gate washed by red dust from the road and black dust from the brake liners.

There might be another route between where I thought I was and the hand-drawn star on the map. Maybe I could wander back roads and get closer, but more likely I was setting up for a "Strange But True" television episode about a once-famous camera monkey being eaten by a cheetah beside an old Jeep empty of fuel. I could almost see the tragic opening credits. Perhaps my identification would be from a half-chewed boot.

I climbed out and pulled on the padlock hanging on the cattle gate. We all do that, right? *Ba-dumm*, it was locked. There was a faint pressed set of wide tire marks leading away in the grass field on the other side. I liked that. Encouraged, I returned to the Willy—and no, I didn't search the fob for a key that might magically, suspiciously open the lock, but instead opened the toolbox in the back at the foot of the jump seat.

I sorted through the hand tools; a hammer, tire iron, wrenches, a pry bar, a pair of vice-grips and screwdrivers, and, *voila*, pressed flat at the bottom of the metal box was a six-inch section of rusted hacksaw blade.

"Ha, a saw," I announced, rhyme unintended but enjoyed.

Placing the blade into the vice-grip teeth, I dialed in the grip until the saw blade was secured. I took to the shackle in the gate hasp with energy and determination. After twenty minutes, my aggressive efforts had managed to produce a slim scratch.

Undeterred, I continued, pumping my arm, sweating from head to toe, not looking up for fear of slicing off a finger or two. I worked away, feeling strong and focused, switching hands and barely pausing—all momentum.

Momentum. I stopped. I blew slight metal fragments from the scratch in the shackle. I stepped back and stared at the cattle gate for a minute before I retrieved my satchel, put my vice-grip saw inside it, and climbed over the steel gate.

The dual set of tire marks turned off to the left some forty yards out in the meadow, which was a large field of green, gently rolling hills. Someone had done a helluva lot of work clear-cutting the jungle. I followed the tire tracks that took me away from the direction of the star on the map. The tire trail skirted the north side of the field, which I realized really was for cattle, after I sank my boot in a cow pie. A fresh, wet cow pie. From then on I followed the path by alternating my eyes from my boots to the trail, which was aimed at a distant out-building and corral in the shade of hundred-foot jungle trees.

My eyes are actually very good, but they do like to play tricks on me. This was part of the joy of being a cinematographer—the delight in the unexpected challenges to visual assumptions.

The caballeros I saw at the side of the corral and seated on the front porch of the outbuilding were all wearing cowboy hats, and they were all midgets. Walking closer, I realized that they were child cowboys, not adults. I also noted that they were not happy little caballeros. Each boy had steel eyes on me. Not one of them spoke as I passed by the corral and front porch and followed my friendly tire marks into a tunnel carved into the jungle.

The five-minute walk in the shade was appreciated. I paused halfway and opened the satchel to see what Titi had put inside. I took out a thermos of cool water and a roll of tortillas and, God bless her life, none of that ghoulish-white cheese. I greedily drank off half of the thermos and continued walking. Stepping back into hot sunlight, I had my next visual surprise.

My first impression? A three-story loaf of bread, if bread was made of sheet metal. The metal sides of the loaf were rusted, and foliage was creeping up high, the jungle attempting to gobble the structure whole. It was an old and neglected airplane hangar.

I followed the tire marks right up to the double-wide rolling steel door, seeing that there were no windows on this end of the building. I hefted the door open and, yay for me, *my* truck was inside, backed in. No sooner did I see the truck than I forgot all about it. I was in a third-world country staring into a three-story airplane hangar filled with a series of detailed, divided movie sets.

A wide panel divided the sets to my left and my right. I recognized the first two from films I had seen on the big screen. The interior of an airplane cabin—economy class. Opposite was a dark alley between two rundown tenement buildings—prime for a noir treatment, before a quaint Italian bistro and restaurant. I continued, slowly, looking into each set, noting how they were accurately detailed and furnished.

I came upon a set I knew intimately; the stairs and hallway of a decrepit and cluttered apartment building. I had been both the director of photography and the Steadicam operator in the film.

The next four extended sets looked good to go, except the film of dust that lay on all surfaces.

Halfway through the enormous soundstage, I gave up on trying to identify movie themes. The sets were clearly not part of a single production, but seemingly random environments, a collection, a collage. There was no story here, not that I could see. Instead, a gathering of sets strung together by an odd, compulsive, high-financed auteur.

I paused in front of the set for *The Loft*, a film Pauline had co-starred in ten years prior as the disheveled mum to a bunch of knife-wielding criminals. There had been several key scenes in the cramped and cluttered apartment kitchen.

Up ahead I saw the staging area of lighting rigs and camera trollies and multiple stacked equipment cases. Everything needed, and more, was ready to go. No expense had been too much; this studio was ready for any scale of production imaginable.

I had walked at least the length of a football field and not seen a soul. Not even an errant cola can or snack wrapper. There was a silence that can only be formed by an immense containment of oxygen. Before I entered the equipment staging area, I stood in front of the last set, still under construction.

If weddings are acts of madness, my ballot was checked. The altar framed the context well—ornate and Gothic and full of black and red and old, dark woods. I was distantly familiar with this set—it was one Pauline had worked in. An over-the-top, finely detailed, and twisted film, which as I recall was based on a selection of Edward Gorey vignettes. I walked past it and moved through the equipment staging area to the door at the end of the soundstage.

Rolling the door far enough to squeeze through, I stepped back out into the heat and light, greeted by a low cloud of hundreds of mean-hearted flies that found my boots and lower pants legs delicious. Except for the dwarf caballeros, I still hadn't seen anyone, and out back was more of the same. I was standing on a roadway of crushed pink gravel that led directly deep inside a tunnel, a canopy of green vegetation. I entered, and while there wasn't a human within sight or earshot, I was not alone. The jungle growth to my sides was alive with scurrying and clicking and rustling. Above, dark birds cackled and took erratic flight. I lowered my eyes and ignored as best I could my entourage of low-flying insects. Stepping back into glaring and hot light, I was looking at a perfectly sensible glass and steel office building—there in the middle of absolutely nowhere within five hundred miles of sanity.

There was a single narrow door with a handprint security device. Stepping up onto the porch, I tried to look inside through the left-side window. It was a no-go. The venetian blinds were drawn. I tried the doorknob and got the expected. For grins, I placed my palm and splayed fingers on the security device. I was rewarded with a pulsing red light. I swept my fingers along the top of the door sill, and the key I knew wouldn't be there wasn't there. I stepped back and gave the door my best impotent scowl. It didn't help.

So I walked to the edge of the crushed pink gravel and found a hefty rock and smashed the side window open.

After squeezing through onto the broken beads of glass on the nice, royal-blue carpet, I stood within a modern and subdued cone of light coming in from above. The air was chilled; I liked that. An alarm was sounding, and I ignored it, but wondered what or who it might bring. That concern didn't have legs, though. My eyes were drawn to a museum display on a one-foot riser. A velvet rope with bunting kept me from entering the display. And that was fine with me.

I have a past affinity for Buick automobiles, predating my enjoyment and hard work on elderly Packards. There was that Midwestern car brand religion that had made me grin. People were lifelong Chrysler or Ford devotees; buying them as a series through their lives not unlike penance. I had briefly adopted the Buick faith and went through a good number of the models until my fervor waned and I stepped back in time and took up tools at Gustin's Restorations.

Now there in the display was a reminder of my long-lost—albeit brief—Buick religion. This automobile was aged, a fine relic worthy of praise and reverence. It took but a moment to place it in the manufacturer's history; it was a land yacht 1966 Buick Electra 225. The absurdly long and elegant vehicle was demolished. As I recalled, the vehicle had gone under the back of an eighteen-wheeler at about 80 mph, and the hood and roof came off like the pull top of a sardine can. The interior was on display, the roof pressed back over the back seats in jagged, angled metal. In the back seat, three children looked to be sleeping and unharmed. The two guys in the front seat had been less lucky; their heads and upper bodies were destroyed. The faux roadway and shoulder in the display was slick with motor fluids, broken glass, auto parts, and a whole lot of blood. Off to the side of the wreck was the half-draped, ruined body and face of the sex bombshell and movie actress Jayne Mansfield.

CHAPTER THIRTEEN

◆ ◆ ◆

RUMBLE SPIN

DEUNG UNLOCKED the door to the left side of his office and entered his museum, crouching just inside to pull on a pair of silk-lined kneepads. He knelt forward on the old, mossy boards of the narrow sidewalk alongside the canal, entering a long-ago era of Venice in the 1900s. Up above, the four stories of rundown shops and houses leaned inward, making the locale claustrophobic. The open doorways and windows were filled with criminals, prostitutes, drunken constables, cruel urchins, all worried and worn out from life.

He knelt his way along the slender boardwalk, passing a fisherman in a dirty panama hat with a line in the foul and still canal water. The fisherman stood under the weak light of a candlelit streetlamp.

Deung looked up as he knelt past, to the tilting houses and shabby shops with pastel-colored signs offering Drugs, Pawning, Fish, and Hats. Twenty yards up, a round, arched bridge crossed the canal. On it was a gang of thugs, a few sitting on the stone rail with their bare feet or battered boots dangling.

Deung looked up over their heads to the tallest building, the listing clock tower with a white smudge face and no hands. The worn boardwalk ended at the base of the bridge, and Deung climbed down into the dark canal water. He waded through pale lily pads and under the dangling feet. The still water was body temperature, and the stones underfoot were oily slick. Deung crossed through the canal to a once colorfully painted gondola tied off to the opposite walkway. Beyond the gondola and walkway was a courtyard and a garden party of sorts in mid-revelry; a gathering of about twenty, all dressed in fancy high-style. These people, like the fisherman and the thugs on the bridge and the prostitutes and criminals and others, were all infants—none older than two years old and all well-preserved; most through taxidermy, but with a few examples of plastination and freeze-drying. The centerpiece of the garden party was a raised dais where Rosalia would eventually reside, once her preservation equipment was upgraded.

Deung knelt his way into the party, nodding and grimacing, depending on who he met. Most of those he looked to had vapid expressions. All of the well-dressed, infant cadavers had double-sized and blank acrylic or glass eyes. As though on cue, music began to play, a *sonata da chiesa* featuring violins and cello. Deung hummed along briefly, making coarse song from his damaged mouth. He looked again to the blank clock tower and frowned.

"Yes, first. A dance," he said to the partiers. They were watching him, pleased and expecting. He began a little dance, enjoying himself until he saw his own face reflected in a milky shop window at the edge of the courtyard. He smacked a waiter, toppling a silver tray of ornate goblets. He crawled past with his lidless eyes raised. At the far edge of the garden party, he removed his knee pads and exited through the shoulder-height door to the next exhibit hall.

There were steep stairs to be climbed and he took them while pinning a gold, six-star sheriff's badge to his baggy, black silk shirt. Deung took a deep breath of clean, cooled air before opening the door to the sickly sweet scents of drinks and sweat and tobacco. Three curation technicians passed by, donning baby-blue surgery suits, rubber gloves, and breathing masks as Deung stepped back to give them room. One of them carried a basket of replacement goblets.

Deung walked into the saloon on the second-floor landing, moving along the narrow row of doors to the whore rooms, taking his first breath of the dusty air. He gazed down over the bannister as he walked the boards to the stairs and scowled into the room at the way it had been rearranged; the saloon was nearly empty; no piano player at the upright, no gamblers at the two poker tables; just three nine-year-old cowboys bellied up at the bar. Two of them had their heads on the rail. The third was staring in Deung's general direction, his double-sized eyes red and blank.

Deung descended the stairs, asking over his shoulder, "What time is it?"

No one answered because no one alive was there.

His saloon hostess was posed before a table with a tray of half-empty glasses. Her wide, dead eyes were to the light coming in from the only window. Deung glanced around the room swiftly before raising the back of her fanciful dress. She wore nothing underneath as usual, and her preteen body had been preserved by plastination, so her skin was soft and pliant. His scarred finger felt for her two most sensitive openings and slid inside both. She didn't respond and didn't resist, and he breathed in her cheaply perfumed shoulder.

He left her, crossed the dusty-planked saloon, and pushed through the swing doors. The sunlight from the lighting rigs above was bright, and the air was foul with the smell of muck. He stepped off the boards and into the mud and worse, and started up Main to the small crowd of western-dressed children gathered at the base of the town's makeshift gallows. He sloshed his way through the crowd and climbed the sidesteps to the boards where a living eleven-year-old caballero was struggling valiantly, panting and calling out from inside his black hood.

Deung ignored the boy and asked, "What time is it?" turning to the handless clock over the bank building.

"I'm calling it high noon," he answered himself and took ahold of the worn wooden lever.

He looked at the black-hooded boy with his thick rope noose.

"You've been judged and sentenced for the violation of my sister," he spoke to the hood. Before there was a response, he pulled the lever and the caballero was launched downward fast, before being choked and snapped short of the ground.

Deung watched the criminal through the open trap door, where the youth was twitching and bobbing and soiling himself.

"Merry final shudders," Deung said. He waited until the last death throe before taking the cleaver saw from the rail and cutting the rope. The body fell into the muddy puddle beside the wooden cart waiting for him. The thin-faced ten-year-old undertaker stood at the cart handles, his expression vacant.

Deung climbed back down the steps, ignoring the watchful, deceased town folk, and followed the path of cattle stench to the hay and feed barn across the way. He walked slowly, scowling down at the mud and filth covering his feet and lower legs. Inside the shade of the barn, Deung undressed on the steel walkway that led to the next exhibit hall. He stepped into the glass shower and rinsed off thoroughly before pulling on the fresh, black silk shirt and pants laid out for him. Along the wall, facing away from the town, was a row of windows offering a view of the dense jungle. Two curation technicians passed him, heading out into main street. One of them carried a black vinyl body bag.

Allister stood with his back to the view, waiting until the techs had left the barn before speaking.

"Well done, Sheriff."

Deung nodded in appreciation, his destroyed face set to stoic and grim resolve. "Gotta do what's right." He accepted the compliment, his damaged tongue adding lisp to the words.

Allister turned away to the windows and cleared his throat.

"How is my Ms. Place?" Deung asked. "Agreeable yet?"

"She's coming around."

"The marriage schedule?"

"We're on schedule. We can begin filming as soon as the set is finished. Two days."

"Not good. You have one day."

Allister nodded and Deung walked way up the corridor to the door to the third exhibit hall.

The door opened to a meadow of ivy in darkness under a sickly gray-and-green-tinged sky. The night, painted on the walls and ceiling, held a crescent moon that cast a white light on the still river and meadow. In the foreground stood a hut made of harsh boards with a ground-level border of lit candles and a single window below a wooden sign that read "Tickets." The air conditioning was circulating the smell of buttered popcorn and faint voices. Deung walked through the ivy to the window and said, "Two, please," placing some coins on the counter.

The teenager inside the booth stared at him with dead eyes, so Deung helped himself to the roll of tickets. Holding two, he walked away to the Rumble Spin, a seven-car Ferris wheel in the center of the meadow. The Rumble Spin was turning, its steel A-frame adorned with rows of small white lights. Most of the gondolas were occupied by teenagers who looked bored. Deung pushed the yellow control button, and the seven gondolas began to slow. When the one with a single occupant cycled down before him, he hit the red button and the car stopped at the base.

"Hey, sis," he said to the partially decomposed but well-done taxidermy of the teenage girl. Opening the little door, he climbed into the gondola and sat beside her. He pushed the green button on the control box that only this car had. He took her hand, which couldn't articulate like those who had received plastination, and held tight as the Rumble Spin glided them up into the night sky.

The gondola cycled to the top and Deung looked down to the small crowd of teens watching him with envious eyes. While the car curved downward, he turned to his sister. Her thick black hair was salon coiffed and marred at the temple, where there was a scorched circle around a dime-sized bullet hole. Her expression was set to a blend of anger and confusion, and her large eyes looked right through him because her head had been poised in that direction. Deung smiled.

"My dear last obstacle," he said to her, reaching over with his free hand and unbuttoning the three top buttons of her blouse.

The gondola cycled twice. As it began its third rise, Deung cupped the teen girl's rigid, full breast and breathed in her perfumed neck.

The Rumble Spin slowly circled four more times. By then, he had her skirt hiked to her belly and his hand up between her dis-colored legs.

"This will have to stop," he told her. "I'm getting married. We will still be able to ride, but no more play."

He took in her forever expression of anger and confusion. She was offering him the appropriate response to his sad news. The car swept low over the ivy and he turned his eyes to the blue-and-black river beyond the meadow. The water was still, and a narrow strip of white lay on it from the backlit moon above.

"Let's lay back," he said, taking his hand from her breast and giving the gondola seat-adjustment bar a pull. The seat back leveled as the car reached the top of the cycle. To assist his sister back meant her stiff lower body and legs would have to rise. A real human voice called out and called out to him.

Deung looked to the gawking crowd of teens posed below, searching for a fresh face. He had to look around to the ticket booth to see Allister, who was shaking his head and waving to him excited-ly. When the Rumble Spin swept his car low, Deung tapped the red button and the gondola stopped, swinging back and forth. He waited until it ceased swinging before opening the short door.

"My apologies, sir," Allister said as he walked up, carrying a black handbag.

"Had me a woody," Deung said sourly, pulling his shirt out over the rise in his silk pants as he stepped down.

"My apologies again, sir. We have an alarm."

"You interrupt for that? What, another critter?"

"No, sir. More serious than that. The alarm shows a window broken in. I've alerted security, but believed you should know."

"Where?"

"The adult exhibit. Back door."

Deung aimed his lidless eyes to Allister's black handbag. "You brought my Judge? Good."

He extended his burn-scarred hand to Allister, who opened the bag and took out the stainless-steel Taurus Judge revolver. He also handed over a box of the .410 hollow-point shotgun-rifled slugs.

Deung took out four of the three-inch bullets and loaded the hand cannon.

"We could let security deal with it," Allister offered, frowning.

Deung ignored the suggestion. "Let's bag us an intruder."

CHAPTER FOURTEEN

♦ ♦ ♦

THE JUDGE

I REMEMBERED seeing the lurid black-and-white photographs in old magazines and newspapers when I was very young. This demolished and peeled-open Buick. The sprawl of the blond bombshell, and the smashed heads and upper bodies of the driver and the guy beside him. She lay in the gravel and scrub weed and was partially exposed and partially covered by a white drop cloth. Climbing over the velvet rope and bunting, I looked into the back seat to Ms. Mansfield's three children. Their clothing and postures had been roughed up in the collision that tossed them around, but they didn't look harmed. The three children looked expressionless or perhaps still sleeping. Their eyes were closed. Their eyelids were closed, stretched, as if covering eyeballs twice the normal size. One of the little darlings had her head tilted back as though dreaming upward, and I looked up as well. Directly above the wreck, a single hot spotlight cast the scene in hard white light. Out beyond, the curved interior walls and ceiling were painted midnight black with tiny stars.

I stepped back. Truth was, I stumbled backward and nearly stepped on a very dead Chihuahua laying in the crash debris and blood and auto fluids just outside the open passenger door.

I was trembling. I was offended. I was starting to glow with anger. Were they real? Or once real? What was this place? What purpose or reason? They had to be fake, right? Like in gaudy wax museums.

I walked further up the anonymous country road, stepping away from the wreck and the harsh cone of light to the next section, fifty yards away.

The next wreck had also been featured in black-and-white tabloid photographs. There was a 1950s two-tone Ford coupe that had been clipped; the front left side was destroyed. Further up the road was the demolished Porsche Spyder that had hit the Ford. There was no one inside the coupe. I walked to Mr. Dean's Porsche, what remained of his once fast and beautiful Spyder. The car was on the shoulder of the road, in the weeds. Like Ms. Mansfield's death scene, this one replicated the cruel photographs. At the rear of the little silver car, a very real-looking James Dean lay in the brush and clutter with his head up. His replicated face was largely undamaged and easily recognized, save the eyes. His expression was sad and twisted with pain and confusion, but his eyes, while resembling the actor's, were twice the size. Another man who must have been in the car with him lay injured and close to his side. I walked away.

There was a third accident up the narrow country road, but I stood still, just outside of the hot light above the last. What kind of offensive madness was this? And why? To what point? Upset and confused, I let my habitual momentum move me up the road, sensing that it was driving me no closer to understanding. I was also beginning to doubt I was getting any closer to finding my wife.

Someone had added the canned sound of crickets, which played while I walked up the pavement in the dark under painted stars. The next spotlight shone on a blackened wreck past a police cruiser with the driver's door open. An officer stood behind the door with his gun aimed at the wreck. I didn't look at his face, or his eyes.

The automobile looked intact, except it was a burnt husk with bullet holes in the trunk. The pavement around the vehicle was scorched, and the car rested on melted tires. It was a convertible of unrecognizable type and was parked before a blockade of three more police cruisers. I stepped to the passenger door and gazed inside. The passenger was likely a woman, because there was a charred purse in her lap. She was burnt beyond any recognition, almost all skin and muscle melted away, revealing black bones in tatters of clothing and skin and ash. Her eyes were open, her eyeballs intact and black and double sized. I looked to the driver. His head and upper body were a chubby pink, untouched by the flames. The driver was grinning. I knew not what for and I couldn't have cared less; what had my gaze was the fact that his eyes were normal sized— the first of these I'd seen in the menagerie of automobile deaths. I looked away. Back up the road to the spot-lit accident scenes. Those displayed the tragic deaths of the famous. If this third accident was of stardom, I didn't know who, but I admitted to not being current on grisly movie star fatalities.

I looked to my right, where a stream of creek water paralleled the road, the water giving off a slight sparkle from the harsh light over the convertible. I followed its widening path further up the road, to where the water widened out beyond the police cruiser barricade. After easing between the cruisers, I continued up. The pavement ended abruptly at an old steel guardrail before a pond, fed from the stream to my right. I climbed over and pressed through the bottle brush to the water's edge. The pond and weeds curved out unevenly to the sides, and some forty yards across the water pressed the three-story wall of the round-topped hangar.

I stepped closer to get a better look, and my knee bumped a sturdy wood table. Looking down, I saw a snorkel tube and an oversized swim mask. Ignoring these, I squinted to the far wall, which was midnight, moonless black except at the center, just over the waterline, where someone had painted an ancient wall before a church of gray stone. There were towers and turrets and a wall across the foreground, including a closed drawbridge. The stonework was ornate and featured many large-eyed gargoyles along the top of the wall, where spikes and vats stood poised at the ready. I stared at the unwelcoming drawbridge and then lower, into the water, where a light of sorts caught my eye. The light was not on the water, but down in its still and patient depth.

The castle and church looked familiar, but I couldn't place them right away. The structure on the black wall was painted in such a way that it appeared a bit hazy and distant; it had been easily a dozen years or more since I last glimpsed the image. The image was also absent of scrolling film credits and sweeping title, but it came to me: this was the castle and church from Pauline's film, *Dark Liaison*, from many years back.

So there I was, staring at a three-story movie poster just beyond a series of ghastly and gruesome car wrecks next to a cocktail table with swimming gear. I turned around, thinking that I could back-track, leave the hangar, and find a way to my wife that would only involve the normal: insects, large carnivores, aggressive birds in the jungle. The other direction was simply bat fucking nuts.

I took one last glance to the castle and church steeple across the water. I looked at that glow from a lightbulb under the surface. There was the little table beside me. Removing my boots, I tied the laces and draped them around my neck.

The water was warm, at least eighty-five tepid degrees. I dunked the swim mask and snorkel to rinse them. The swim mask was set for a larger head than mine, so I adjusted it and mouthed the snorkel. The water tasted oily and carried the scent of lavender, of all things.

Sure, why not, I thought, looking around. Lowering into the still, black water, I pushed off and swam slowly to the center of the pond.

I dunked my head and checked my bearing on the light in the water. It was five feet under the surface and looked like a standard domed pool light. Swimming to the wall, I knocked on it and received the hollow sound of wood. The painted castle and church above were waiting for me, so I took a big gulp of air and dove.

Under the light dome there was an opening, and I swam low enough to see inside. There was a string of the lights in a tunnel.

I surfaced and gave myself one last chance to stop my *momentum* before taking a deep breath and diving again.

The tunnel was four lights long, each ten feet apart. I didn't linger but also didn't panic, clearing the mouth at the opposite side of the tunnel and swimming up for the surface.

I've seen many wonderful and very strange scenes. After all, I was in the movie business. Not counting the craziness of the autos and the dead children and the castle painting I'd just left, what I was looking at was truly bent. And familiar.

There was Pauline's *Viewfinder*, a replica for sure, floating at anchor in the calm, scented waters of a movie-set pool under harsh filming lights. The sixty-foot boat had been modified and decorated. The modifications were for filming. There were two units of cameras, mounted light rigs, and the usual boom mics. One was on the stern, facing into the salon. The second was forward, directly over and aimed down into the cutaway roof above Pauline's stateroom.

The *Viewfinder* was adorned with white potted flower displays; Pauline's favorite white lilies. Treading water, I simply gawked, with enough presence of mind to note that there was no one on board. The soundstage walls were covered with hundreds of bolted mattresses, even up above along the curved ceiling. There was a walkway around the pool wall, and I considered swimming to the side and climbing out. Instead, I swam to the boat, to the transom and swimming platform. I climbed out and stood beside the transom with the accurately reproduced boat's name, *Viewfinder*, painted on the fine wood. Taking ahold of the ladder rungs, I started to climb, but stopped. I heard voices.

Two men were in clipped conversation, moving in my direction and out of view—the boat was between them and me. The voices drew closer, moving alongside the boat. I heard other boots enter the soundstage; one of the men near me ordered, "Search the other side."

Put my hands up, paste on a regretful expression, and offer myself up? I was starting to piece together my first words when the two men stepped into view. I dropped the half-formed explanation. The first was a handsome, silver-haired man in a business suit. He was talking into a radiophone, one stride behind the ugliest man I had ever seen; a short man, viciously scarred, who held an oversized silver handgun. There was a shout at my back, and this guy looked past me first, to the others circling the *Viewfinder*. Then he spotted me, with his lidless eyes. I raised one hand, the other holding on. He lifted and aimed the gun. And pulled the trigger.

I'm not sure how, but I believe the barrel spat out a nine-inch flame when it fired. There was no pain at first. I was knocked backward from the swimming platform. Landing in the water, I spun, got my bearings, and dove under. Stroking with my hands and kicking my legs, my body felt all wrong. Broken and disjointed and yet moving. I aimed for the tunnel. There still wasn't any pain yet. Only a distant sense of harm. Once I entered the glow of the first light dome, I stopped. I hadn't gotten a full breath and didn't have time to linger, but I paused long enough to see the smoky swirls of my blood in the white light.

CHAPTER FIFTEEN

◆ ◆ ◆

WEDDING BED

THE *VIEWFINDER* replica was moored in the center of the Deung's fifty-meter pool. The boat's keel had been removed because it was no more needed than the twin Chrysler engines needed fuel. Deung stood parallel to the stern of the boat, looking at his wrist, which was torqued by the firing of the Judge. The gun had made an absurdly loud boom that was only muffled by the water and the hundreds of mattresses on the soundstage walls.

"That hurt me," he said to the gun, admonishing it.

Deung extended the Judge behind his back, and Allister relieved him of it.

Deung looked across the water to his three security guards, crouched and wide-eyed, with their guns out of their holsters.

"Search it," he said, pointing to the *Viewfinder*. He saw the spray of blood on the transom lettering.

The three guards lowered themselves into the water and swam to the boat as Deung squatted and pulled the tow line that drew the dinghy to him. It had been fitted with a 5hp trolling motor, and Deung cruised across the pool, meeting with the guards at the swimming platform. He frowned. There was little blood.

He pointed to the ladder, still frowning, and the first guard climbed. When the other two were aboard, Deung followed. He remained at the back rail, letting them go forward, weaving through the white floral displays and the guests already aboard.

The guests were posed and looking pleased. Most sat on the deck benches, but a few stood on their own, the aluminum support bars barely visible. It was a nice gathering of well-dressed, unknown faces, and a few that had once been familiar and famous; all stiff and stuffed and looking happy, their large eyes bright with delight. Deung had worked the guest list carefully for the wedding reception. One of the famous was a peer of Pauline's. He had tried to dig up others.

While the guards entered the salon and continued the search, Deung called across to Allister, "Who was that?"

Allister was studying the blood cloud in the wavering pool water at the rear of the *Viewfinder*.

"No idea. We'll pull him out and see."

Deung ducked around the camera and tripod mounted to the stern and looked out to the water. The surface was dancing and shimmering and bloodstained.

"Is that a lot of blood?" he called.

"Yes," Allister answered.

Deung stepped around a lighting mount and looked to the salon doors for his guards. He could hear them calling tersely to one another as they searched the boat.

"It was a white guy. Not a local," Deung shouted to Allister. "Any ideas?"

"No, sir."

"I don't like that answer."

From inside the short hall one of the guards called out, "*Borra todo*," giving the all clear.

The three soaked guards came out through the salon door in single file and stood among the guests looking uncertain, with their eyes avoiding the standing and sitting dead.

"Did you disturb my wedding bed?' Deung asked. "Never mind—I'll look."

He entered the salon, crossed to the galley, and went down the steps. The other compartment doors were closed, but the stateroom door stood open. He stepped in to the foot of the bed. Light and air were entering from the opening in the ceiling where the cameras, boom mics, and lights were at the ready. The room was a festival of white lilies and looked undisturbed. Deung went back topside.

He walked past the reception guests and his guards and climbed over the back rail on the ladder, speaking just before lowering from view, "You three find the intruder. Shouldn't be difficult."

With that, he cautiously climbed into the dinghy and motored across to where Allister stood ready to assist.

Deung climbed up with some difficulty, rolling on the concrete and pedaling his legs to stand. Allister offered a hand and it was waved away.

"Call your boy, that Ethan, and make sure my Pauline is okay," Deung ordered. "Place more security with her," he added.

Allister dialed his radiophone and Deung looked back to the pool where his three guards were treading water before dunking under to chase down the intruder.

CHAPTER SIXTEEN

◆ ◆ ◆

BLOOD IN THE WATER

SHRIEKING ALARMS filled my brain. I swam past the last light globe in the tunnel. My arms and legs hadn't been hit, and I worked them hard as possible. When my feet found purchase on the mossy stones, I stood and searched my head and chest and neck for wounds.

I was wild with fear, surely in shock.

"I've been shot." My body was shaking from head to toe.

My fingertips found the hole low on my ribs. I raised that hand to my eyes. It was soaked with my own blood. I pressed the wound that I still didn't feel. I didn't look down. I felt my blood cover that hand. Sliding my hand to my back, smearing my skin, I found the spot where the bullet had exited my body—just off center on my back.

Sucking a deep breath brought a wave of pain. I needed to scream with each breath. Tearing off the swim mask and snorkel, I tossed them and stared at the guard rail. Climbing up onto the bank, brushing through the tall grass and cattails, I didn't stop until I was up on the pavement.

The chaotic flickering of my thoughts began to slow.

There's a bullet hole in me, came first.

Am I going to die today? came next, while I made my way to the two police cruisers.

My body was trembling; I coughed, wiping my mouth with my clean hand. I looked at it. No blood. I assumed that was good.

I had no plan as I eased between the nose-to-nose police cars. I instinctively moved away from that gun and its owner. My boots were heavy, full of water, and I took them from around my neck and dropped them. Coughing, shaking, I approached that burnt-to-the ground convertible.

I stared at the driver, the only object in the car that wasn't charred or blackened. I opened his door and leaned in. The skin of his face was real; pores, shaving nicks, fine eye lashes. Real or realistic, I didn't know. Or care. I watched his steady eyes while I unbuttoned his shirt.

He had the flabby chest and soft skin of someone who avoided exercise. More of his upper body was revealed while I removed his shirt. I planned to use it to somehow bind the two holes in my body. I was stepping back when I saw the gun holster on his hip. I didn't pause to reflect. I took the gun out of the holster.

Before I unfurled the shirt to make a tourniquet, I placed the black handgun on the trunk of the car.

I didn't know if the tourniquet was helpful or the right thing to do, but it freed up a hand, which I wiped off with the shirt tail. Taking the gun in that same stained hand, I headed off, retreating from the tunnel and Pauline's boat and that ugly, scarred man with his own gun. I *had* to get as far away as I could from the men with guns. I started up along the lonely two-lane, trembling, coughing, walking barefoot, as quickly as possible.

James Dean's sad, confused, pained expression took on a new reality as I passed by him. I was empathetic like never before. I moved past him and the old Ford his Porsche had clipped, starting him on his own path to fear and darkness and, in his case, death. I kept moving forward. Moving was good.

I thought of taking the white cloth that covered most of Jayne Mansfield's body, but it would be too large, and the shirt binding my wounds was stemming the spill of my blood. Tightening the tourniquet, I looked at the spray of glass shards and considered turning around for my boots. The outdoor light coming in through the broken window was more persuasive. A path out of the soundstage. I heard voices, movements from behind, and ditched the idea of my boots. I crossed the broken glass and climbed outside.

Out in the heat and bright daylight, the flying insects found me fast. Men were shouting inside the building. I moved my legs up along the pink gravel path. Beyond, way beyond, was a meadow and a cattle gate and the Willy.

More voices carried from inside that three-story hangar. I walked as best I could, hurrying. Men were calling out to one another in Spanish.

I raised the handgun in my awkward left hand and turned around. I aimed it at that broken window.

I'd had a good amount of experience with handguns and rifles. Unfortunately, all movie props. What were the odds that the gun I held was real, considering where I found it? And if it was real, what were the chances it was loaded?

I backed away before turning around, entering the green brush and shade.

Those three voices became crisp and loud as they approached. I lowered to my knees, which hurt like hell, and choked off another demanding cough. I searched the vegetation I had just moved through. I didn't see any blood on the leaves or the dark soil. The voices drew closer. I hunched low and ducked my head.

Their boots crunched on the gravel, moving past. I looked up. Three caballeros with handguns, walking side by side. Warm fluid, had to be blood, was climbing up my throat. I needed to stand up; there was too much pain.

Stepping deeper into the jungle, I found a dense spot that hid me well, and I decided I'd wait them out. Let them look everywhere—well, almost everywhere. Make my way to the Willy. Drive the Jeep to Sara at Pauline's villa, light up the radio with calls to the *policia, federales*, whatever. Even the embassy, if there was one. Then get myself to a hospital. If there was one.

All I had to do was be patient and not cough when those three were nearby. Maybe wait until dark to make my escape.

The insects feasted. I had a spell of the shakes and decided to lay down. Let the flying carnivores have their way with my skin, as long as I kept quiet.

"Can I survive this?" Probably contracting malaria before getting help with the gunshot wound, but I'd get treated. I lay my head back on the dirt and rested the gun on my chest and closed my eyes.

CHAPTER SEVENTEEN

◆ ◆ ◆

WEDDING MARCH

"YOUR BRIDE is en route," Allister said to Deung.

With that news, Deung made his way back through the museum to the front office, Allister one stride back. They didn't exchange a word until they were inside the building, when Allister asked Deung for the large handgun. "I'll put it away."

"No," Deung barked. He walked to his desk where his tux was draped.

As Deung undressed, Allister looked away and placed another call, to the nominal leader of the three security guards. There was no answer. His third call was to Rolf on the film set.

"AP," she answered briskly, professionally.

"It's Allister. How are we?"

"Chaos, but under control. The set is finished, and we've started a full crew walkthrough."

"Good. We're heading over—"

Deung shoved Allister's arm and said, "Let's get the wedding over fast. I want my wedding night."

Allister ended the call and followed Deung through his half mansion. As they entered the main hall, Allister waved off the staff and employees hurrying from the side halls. Deung stepped out into the shade of the portico, his staff evenly lined up to his left and right. Deung stood in the shadows, looking down the wide steps. A gold golf cart was crossing the lawn to the right. He watched as it came to a stop at the base of the stairs.

Ethan was driving. A nurse in blue uniform sat in back, beside Pauline, who wore an elegant white wedding gown. The nurse had her arms out, holding Pauline in place. Ethan climbed out and he and the nurse assisted the bride from her seat. Her head and face were covered with a white lace veil.

Deung took one step down.

"Bad luck, sir," Allister admonished in careful voice.

Deung growled and stepped back up.

Three members of the house staff descended the stairs to delicately help the bride as Pauline appeared around the back of the golf cart. Deung saw her uncertain footing, one of her white slippers dragging in the coral gravel. He turned away and went back through his half mansion, heading for the altar on the soundstage.

Allister followed.

"Sir, if I may? A best man. Have you decided?"

Deung raised one of his ruined fingers. "Let's use my dad."

Allister raised his radiophone. "We're gonna need to move Deung Senior to the film set. Get him into a tux."

By the time Deung and Allister entered the business office, employees in blue surgery suits had lowered Deung Senior onto a rolling gurney and were changing the elderly cadaver into the wedding tux.

"Big day," Deung said to his mum, ignoring the workers.

"Big night too," he added, groping his scrotum before leaving the room.

He and Allister retraced their way through the museum and across the path to the studio building. The film set was a beehive of activity as the various crews hastened to put the final touches on the altar and take their positions at the lights, audio boards, and cameras. An RV had been driven into the soundstage and parked against the side wall of mattresses. Deung walked to it.

"Your script is on the table," Allister reminded gently.

Deung didn't reply. Allister got the door.

Deung stepped up into the elegant and modern vehicle. He looked the sterile room over, thoughts elsewhere.

"The ring," he demanded.

Allister handed him the black ring box.

Deung opened it with his scarred fingers and nodded. "Very bloody. Nice."

He raised the ring to his lidless eyes and examined the three-carat blood diamond. "I hope she'll be delighted," he said. Allister accepted the empty box and looked away as Deung pocketed the ring.

"Let me know when the movie crew and my bride are ready," Deung instructed, pointing Allister to the door.

Allister entered the set, a busy gathering of the director, the cinematographer, and assistants. He took a spare canvas chair set back a ways. Taking his phone off his belt, he watched the movie makers work in their heated, focused preparations. Allister dialed the security lead, and the man started to explain. Allister listened for twenty seconds.

"Did you *really* try to find that guy?" he interjected. "Keep searching."

Out on the set, a hush fell as all heads turned.

Pauline Place was being escorted across the soundstage. At least a vestige of Pauline Place, her face veiled and her wedding slippers fumbling. She was held upright by two nurses on each side with Ethan in tow, lifting the gown's train.

"What the hell?" Rolf yelled, offended.

Heads turned and Allister followed their gaze from the famous actress. It was Deung Senior being rolled on a dolly in their direction. Pauline was eased onto a chair, and Deung Senior was rolled past her, up to his position just to the side of the altar. The assistants secured him, adjusting the aluminum support work at the back of the cadaver. One of the assistants twisted his head toward the spot where his son would be taking his marriage vows. His lower arms were adjusted so that his leaf-colored hands joined, with some difficulty, at his lower belly. The assistant worked quickly, averting her eyes from Deung Senior's newly delighted expression and the bullet hole in his forehead.

Rolf slipped away from the film crew and cameras and walked to Allister, who still sat in his canvas chair, watching the production with a distasteful scowl.

"We're ready. Call him," she said.

"No." Allister kept his eyes on the spectacle that was fully lit for filming. "The pews are empty."

"And?"

"He wants his audience. Witnesses, if you prefer."

Allister turned and they both looked past Pauline, who was being held upright in her chair.

"Aw, jeez," Rolf breathed.

Caster wheels were rolling as assistants wheeled in familiar faces and outfits. Most of the dead children were from the canal scene, the others from the garden party.

Allister and Rolf watched in silence as the young bodies were rolled to the two rows of pews, unloaded, and put in place, half on the bride's side and half for the groom.

When the young cadavers were all settled in, Allister stood. "I'll go get our happy groom."

"Allister, none of my business," Rolf asked, "but isn't she still married?"

"Messy detail. We have a sharp legal team."

"And?"

"She signed. Sort of. Wasn't in the room at the time."

"Oh, good. Glad this disgusting nightmare is *legal*."

Rolf walked back to the film crew as Allister crossed to the RV and knocked twice.

The door opened and Deung descended the metal steps with a resplendent smile, his eyes to the altar. He crossed, his gaze averted from his soon-to-be bride, and spoke only one time as he entered the aisle between the pews: "She has my ring, right?"

Allister froze midstride and muttered, "Oh fuck," then answered, "Yes, we're on it."

He looked away from the cameras to Ethan, off to the left side, and pantomimed a ring sliding onto his finger.

Ethan went flush. He let go of Pauline Place's shoulder and ran for the exit.

Rolf hollered, "We go in two. Check in."

From different vantage points voices called out:

"Cameras. Check."

"Sound. Check."

"Light. Check."

An upright piano began to play Mendelssohn's "Wedding March." Deung had eschewed the common use of an organ. A hefty amount of reverb was effecting the piano notes, adding some of the grandeur and bombast that an organ would readily provide.

Allister backed up the aisle and entered the groom-side pew, second row, leaning back from the bodies in the front row. He turned to the bride, who was lifted to her feet and slowly assisted forward through the audience toward the altar. Her white beaded veil was nodding up and down slowly.

Pauline Place was swept along past Allister's row. His eyes followed her and then beyond, to Deung, who stood in his fine black tuxedo, looking reverently to her, standing there beside his proud, dead father.

Cameras were rolling. Pauline's gown and veil went electric white as she entered the full lights on the altar. The nurses bent over to stay out of camera range as best they could while turning the actress around to face her soon-to-be.

Allister was the first to notice that something was missing. He sat and dug out his radiophone quickly, dialed, and whispered harshly, "*Where is my priest?*"

Looking up, he saw that Deung was also aware of the error. His lidless eyes and furrowed, scarred brow were aimed at Allister, his upper lips pulled back in an angry grimace.

Rolf must have seen the exchange and yelled, "Cut."

Deung bellowed, "No cut."

The cameras continued to roll—the crew in rare defiance of the AP, fearing the man with the immense checkbook.

There was shuffling and scurrying from stage right as an assistant carried a white step stool to the altar, and two others entered the harsh lighting, rolling the priest on a handcart.

Allister stared. He had seen this before during rehearsals, but the use of the tall, gaunt, eleven-year-old boy was difficult to look away from. The youth wore a white papal gown and white triangulated cap. Death had discolored his face and hands to a dry gray. The priest's jaw had been cut and modified specifically for the service and the incisions ran from both of his ears to his lips. Like Deung Senior, the eleven-year-old priest was held upright by a working of aluminum posts. The assistants transferred him from the handcart to the white step stool. When he was steady, one of them eased around behind the cadaver and climbed up inside its white gown.

The unseen piano player began another rendition of the "Wedding March." The elevated boom mics lowered over the bride, groom, and priest as the cameras rolled. Deung turned his pleased eyes to Pauline's veil.

When the last piano note struck, there was a moment of silence. Movement from off set caught Allister's attention and he glanced away, to the three security guards walking over, their uniforms soaking wet and their expressions sheepish.

"Fucknuts didn't find him," he breathed and turned his attention back to the movie set.

The priest's gown was rustling as the assistant inside got into position. Deung scowled at the priest and grunted.

"Start it *now*," he demanded.

The words of the ceremony began to carry from the speakers. The aide inside the priest reached up and articulated his jaw and mouth, pantomiming the words of the service.

Allister turned around, looking for Ethan and the groom's ring. No luck. He looked again to the altar and the spectacle in the hot lights.

The priest was *talking* and Deung was nodding along, keeping his eyes to his bride's veiled face.

Allister's radiophone hummed. He glanced at its display and saw the name "Tacas," who was coordinating the wedding night preparations. He didn't take the call.

The priest was drawing to a close—Allister was familiar with the soundtrack. He watched Deung take the wedding ring from his pocket. The priest paused. Deung announced his, "I do," and reached out to Pauline Place.

His disfigured fingers carefully, gently raised her veil, tenderly rolling it back on her head and hair.

And there she was. Beautiful, famous, adored Pauline Place. Her eyes shifted and her head tilted back and away slowly as she took in her surroundings.

Deung's hands eased back from her head, and he extended the wedding ring. The priest spoke directly to Pauline. She watched the eleven-year-old's jaw work with the few simple words. She raised her fine chin and opened her eyes wide.

Deung cut in.

"Let's call that her 'I do.'"

Pauline Place's eyes swept from the gray-skinned priest to the burn-scarred Deung.

She swayed. She made a *kaa*-ing sound that rose in volume. Then she began to scream.

CHAPTER EIGHTEEN

♦ ♦ ♦

SIXTEEN BULLETS

I LAY in green shadows on dark brown dirt. My body was involuntarily shaking; shock, I believed. My clothing was wet. Blood and water. No shoes. No satchel. But I did have the 9mm resting on my chest. I listened to the three well-armed thugs. They entered the jungle tunnel to the movie studio beyond. I lay as still as I could for ten minutes. The sounds of their boots and voices did not return. Before I sat up, I cinched the borrowed shirt tighter around my wounds. This was painful but stemmed some of the bleeding.

When I sat up fully, pain arced up inside my body like lightning. My thoughts and vision wobbled, but I didn't stop and pushed on, propping myself with my arms. I looked out to the pink gravel path before I rose to my feet. I began to *see* my plan.

I would skirt the movie studio and stay out of view. Having the 9mm added some bravery. I'd move slow and sneaky through the jungle and parallel to the building. Do the same around the corral and those stiff caballeros. Stay in the overgrowth along the cow meadow. Then the Willy and the roads.

Spot and wave down the authorities. Then search for a hospital or a doctor's office. No. Going to Pauline's villa was a better plan. There was the doctor that was helping Sara. And the radios. Raise a firestorm with them soon as I figured out how they worked. A military and police rescue of Pauline. And shut down this sick amusement park.

A good idea and plan.

I brushed through the foliage out onto the pink gravel. Off to my right was the tunnel I had to move through before sneaking past the studio building and the corral. Looking into the tunnel and standing still, I scanned for the movement of those three with their guns. Entering that enclosure looked dangerous, but I'd stay to the side, ready to hide and crouch in the plants and shadows if they appeared.

I gripped the 9mm tight in my hand and stared at the pink path leading up through the tunnel. I saw the wash of sunlight in the clearing at the other end.

I wondered if they would use helicopters to rescue Pauline.

That would speed up saving her.

Had to remember to demand helicopters.

Time was crucial.

I looked back in the opposite direction.

Time was crucial and Mr. Momentum was retreating?

I stepped out into the heat and painfully bright sunlight.

And turned to Pauline.

◆ ◆ ◆

LEAVING THE path to that sick museum where I had been shot, I walked out into the clear-cut meadow. I started across calmly and quickly, aiming for the cover of growth across the way. I saw how I could use the growth and shadows to make my way to the front of the compound. I suspected that if there was a main house, that's where I'd find my wife.

I had the gun to at least aim and threaten with until I got my hands on a radiophone and called in help.

Moving as quickly as possible, I crossed that low grass clearing as best I could. Blood loss was surely affecting my brain, but I stayed with my decision, keeping Mr. Momentum aimed forward.

To my left across the way was the side of the movie studio building, and I think I saw the roof of other structures in the high treetops. I now had a target and entered the jungle to make the long turn.

Stepping into the shade and cool moist air of the vegetation, there was movement to my left. I froze in place and gripped the 9mm. And stared.

My old travel chum, Ethan, was starting across the clearing, walking a pink path away from the studio building. I stood perfectly still as he crossed the field and disappeared. Then I moved out. Not for the residence, but to follow him.

I paused only once. It took two minutes to check out the handgun worked without shooting myself. Or a tree.

Oh Lordy, it was loaded.

I figured out how to release the clip from inside the handle and saw it could hold sixteen bullets. *Sixteen* bullets. I didn't know how many it actually held, but the clip felt heavier than it looked, and a real-looking bullet was at the ready at the top. I put the clip back inside the gun and turned the safety switch, having no idea if I had turned it on or off.

Pulling the trigger would tell, if I had to do that. Didn't seem likely. I was headed for young, pince-nez-wearing Ethan, whom I suspected was as fearful of real weapons as I was.

The path he had walked entered an opening in the wall of green. I made that turn. I could have stopped and gawked, but a new slice of pain like a shard of glass dug into my side and back.

A white-tiled swimming pool was centered on a lawn. The water was translucent. Hundreds of white lilies in white vases surrounded the rectangle of blue. A path also adorned with lilies led to a bungalow. It was white, too, even the roof. There was a double glass door in the shade of the porch, and it was open on one side.

I was almost to the porch when Ethan appeared. He was holding something small in his hand and looked surprised, *very* surprised to see me. His eyes lowered from mine to my body. He blinked.

"Don't you have enough of her ashtrays?" I asked.

My voice was both husky and liquid. Like the air from my lungs was wet.

He didn't answer my first question, so I gurgled another.

"Where's my wife?"

His eyes widened frog-like so that the ridiculous pince-nez looked tinier than usual. Those same eyeglasses roamed from the side of my body to the 9mm. He put the object in his pocket, sucked in a breath, and finally formed some words.

"She's no longer your wife."

"Oh?" I paused and let that news sink in.

I stared at him and he focused on the gun.

I finally spoke. "Okay, so where is my ex-wife?"

The pince-nez elevated and aimed beyond me. "In the chapel," he said.

"Chapel?" It was all I could muster.

"She's remarrying."

"Wow. Even in the *industry*, that's fast. Take me there."

He flinched and looked uncertain. I delighted in how persuasive aiming a gun at someone's face was.

Ethan started back along the path, past the swimming pool. I followed him with the 9mm aimed at him. We didn't talk as we retraced his steps back across the clearing.

Instead of moving south toward those rooftops showing above and through the trees, Ethan headed for a door in the side of the building directly across.

"The wedding's in there?" I asked.

"Yes, and you don't want to see it. You won't be welcome, either."

"What? I'm not on the guest list? I'm famous for crashing parties."

"So I've read."

"Keep walking." I coughed.

Being out in the stunning daylight and heat was painful, but the scents of the jungle—sour and dank and rot—were not missed. I waved the 9mm. Ethan opened the door, and we looked into black darkness. There was an onrush of cool, air-conditioned air.

I grabbed his arm and held him back.

"You were in on this since we met?" I asked.

"Way before, yes."

"On me, like a leech," I said to the darkness inside the doorway.

"A *leech*?" Ethan responded with distaste.

"So, who's behind this madness? Who do you work for?"

"The groom."

"He owns this nuthouse." It wasn't a question.

"He owns a lot more."

"Blood sucking leech." I coughed again, to jab him. It worked. His face was crunched up like he had sipped rotten milk. I felt a bit better.

"And why?" I asked. "And don't give me that *access* bullshit."

"I cherish your ex—I mean, Pauline Place."

"No. *I cherish her.* What you are is dog fucking mad."

He looked like he had taken a second drink of fowl chunky milk. I smiled, even with the pain and bloody shirt darkening around myself.

"Try again," I said.

"Mr. Deung—that's the groom. He and I… We're both collectors."

"Collectors?"

"Well he's on a much grander scale, but—"

"And Pauline's role in this…collecting?" I cut him off. "Not exactly willing, I'm gonna bet."

"No, well, she's an icon, a rarity, a—"

"She's a woman. And a mom. And good to her friends. And just so happens to work in bright lights."

"No, she's much more. She's an artist, a trailblazer, a—"

"I so want to put a bullet in you."

I sensed he wanted to share a litany of effusive blabber. While I might agree with it, it wasn't exactly the time.

"Lead the way," I said.

He nodded to the gun barrel, and I followed him into the cool air.

My vision struggled to adjust to the darkness of the sound-stage, which was quiet save some low voices and the roll and squeak of wheels.

Ethan and I stood side by side, squinting. I made out the source of the rolling wheels. Fully loaded handcarts and dollies were being rolled away from the movie set and into the shadows beyond.

The movie set in the distance was lit by a single tower lamp, although others were in place. That one lamp lit the cameras, trollies, booms, and equipment trunks. The set itself was that eerie, faux church interior and altar I had seen before. There were men and women moving about the set. tearing down the filming equipment and crating it.

"Looks like we're too late," Ethan explained the obvious.

An upright piano rolled past us.

"I'm confused," I said. "Was this a wedding or a film production?"

"It was both."

"And the bride, my ex, went along with this?"

"Sort of."

"Explain 'sort of.'"

"She—Pauline Place—was medicinally persuaded. The ceremony also ensured your sons' protection."

I spat on the ground.

"Now I *really* want to put a bullet in you. But first, where is she now?"

"It's her wedding night."

Forming my next question, my mid-body exploded in startling pain. I gasped and collapsed, recoiling from the blow. Ethan had punched me right in the center of my bloody wound.

Crashing to the ground, groaning, I rolled and got up a bit sideways on my two shaky knees. He was running deeper into the soundstage.

The danger and risk of handguns is having them nearby when in hot emotion. Emotions like fear and revenge. In this case the emotion was anger.

I aimed and pulled the trigger once. Then four or five times. I didn't count.

I pulled the trigger one more time and looked at the 9mm in my hand.

"Whaddaya know, it's real."

CHAPTER NINETEEN

— ◆ ◆ ◆ —

SPANISH BOLERO

ALLISTER FOLLOWED Deung and Pauline Place, keeping two strides back to avoid stepping on the actress's gown. Two nurses walked alongside Pauline, assisting the newly remarried movie star.

The actress began to crumble, but was caught as the wedding party departed the studio building and stepped out into the pressing heat and humidity and fierce daylight. Members of the film crew jogged past. A man stood at the end of the crushed-coral path, holding the museum side door open.

Once inside the cool air and dim lights, Allister waited for his eyes to adjust while following the newlyweds to the second and final movie set. Someone was rolling a wood walkway to the side of the large pool. Rolf and the film crew were busy about the cameras, light rigs, and audio equipment. Members of his own team were transferring a few of the select *guests* from the wedding scene, positioning the cadavers among the other finely dressed dead on the stern deck of the replica of Pauline Place's boat, the *Viewfinder*.

"A night of delicious magic," Deung whispered to his wife.

Her nurses guided her up the ramp and across to her yacht. She was helped aboard and put in place among the guests, in the center of the reception. The nurses turned her so that her gaze was through the cadavers to the stern and the view of the open ocean beyond.

Rolf eased through the extended booms and cameras and approached Pauline. Her gaze had drooped again, so Rolf gently raised her head and adjusted the movie star's posture with a deft touch to her shoulders and a nudge upward to her chin. Taking a tissue from her pocket, Rolf dabbed away a trail of drool from the side of the beautiful actress's lips. Stepping back and studying the wedding party as a whole, Rolf called out, "In two."

"That's my cue," Deung said to Allister.

As rehearsed, Allister reached over the pool wall and secured the dinghy for his boss to climb into. When Deung was aboard, Allister untied the rubber craft and cast it off gently. Deung started the trolling motor but didn't put it in gear.

Allister looked across the water to the tightly packed movie equipment and crews on the boat. Behind the bride and the posed guests, the offensively bright lights were being dimmed, casting the tableaux in a warm, romantic glow. He saw the nurses duck from view and knew they were kneeling and holding Pauline Place upright.

"Check in," Rolf hollered.

The three crews for lights, cameras, and audio called out their "Go" status, crisp and loud.

"In one," Rolf commanded.

That was Deung's second cue. He put the trolling motor in gear and steered to the far end of the filming pool. At the same time, a large but silent machine activated, and the "ocean" water began to undulate, causing Deung's dinghy and the water between him and the *Viewfinder* to rise and fall in fairly realistic swells.

Deung leaned over cautiously and splashed water aggressively back up onto himself. His head and clothing were soaked, and he was back in position when Rolf started the film.

"Roll!"

Allister watched Deung "bravely cross dangerous" waters as scripted.

He took out his radiophone and dialed Ethan for a status on the wedding ring, whispering to himself, "He should be back by now."

He listened as the call rang and rang. An incoming call displayed. Placing the call to Ethan on hold, he accepted the other call, identified as "Tacas."

"Yes," Allister said.

"I assume you didn't hear it. There've been gunshots, in the other building. We'll find out what that's about and let you know."

"Yes, do." He ended that call. He saw Ethan's line was still ringing and ended that call as well.

Deung made an aggressive, tight turn at the *Viewfinder's* transom and climbed quickly, confidently, up the ladder and onto the deck. The cameras pivoted. He struck a gallant pose among the gathering of guests with their discolored skin and proud or happy expressions and delighted, oversized eyes.

From where Allister stood at the pool wall, the groom and his bride appeared from chest up, above the deceased children. He looked at Pauline for a moment, then clenched his jaw and looked away.

Deung moved to his waiting bride. Because the nurses were out of sight, it looked like she raised and extended her hand of her own volition. Deung took her arm and she was turned. The married couple sauntered through the reception to the open salon door. When they had stepped inside, the fine wooden door closed.

"Cut," Rolf yelled.

Like ants in a kicked mound, the film crew dispersed from the equipment and scurried forward on the boat, along the narrow walkway on both sides of the salon. Within a minute they were in place at the second unit, including the dual cameras mounted on extension rigs and aimed straight down through the cutaway ceiling above the marital bed.

The crews made final adjustments and waited for Rolf's direction. The newlyweds strolled at leisure through the salon, the squatting nurses assisting Pauline past the guests with their admiring eyes. Allister watched the couple pass the last salon window and out of view. He looked forward to the bow of the boat, with its cameras and lights.

With the wedding party all on board, the crew turned off the swell-forming equipment, and the "ocean" around the *Viewfinder* calmed. All exterior lighting was cut so that the strong white lights over the marriage bed shone ever brighter.

Music began on cue, carrying from speakers on tripods. It was a sultry piece played by a quintet at a heartbeat pace, over single timpani. With each slow round of melody, the pace slightly quickened.

The song carried across the smooth pool water.

"I can't recall the title," Allister whispered to himself, turning from the final scene.

"It's 'Dos Gardenias,'" someone whispered at his back. "If that helps."

CHAPTER TWENTY

◆ ◆ ◆

CRASH THE PARTY

I WATCHED Ethan sprawl forward, his head smacking a white footstool at the altar, splashing it with his own blood. Walking to him, I saw the bullet hole in the back of his head, just under his left ear. Most of the bullets I had fired had, of course, missed, but a second had struck him in the upper back.

Having killed someone was about as sad and painful as being shot myself.

I looked away, walking from the faux church in the midst of moviemaking equipment.

Outside, I started my search for the residence, maybe in one of those buildings in the jungle to the south. I walked halfway along the side of the first building, and stopped. Music played from inside. There was a door, and I had the 9mm. I changed my plan.

The door opened to a short, dark hall and a black curtain that I parted. A man was standing at the pool wall that contained the mockup of Pauline's *Viewfinder*. I saw a film crew working on the bow. As I approached the man, offensive, dead faces up on the stern deck came into view. I listened to him comment on the music, as if that's all that was going on.

"I can't recall the title," Allister whispered to himself, turning from the final scene.

"It's 'Dos Gardenias,'" I whispered at his back. "If that helps."

He turned, at first looking like he appreciated the information. Instead of using the 9mm, I grabbed his neck. He was the tall and thin man with silver hair I had seen before. I jammed his head forward, bending him over, his arms floundering to fight me off.

I held his head underwater for more than minute, his legs kicking and his arms flailing. I kept his head submerged until his futile struggles weakened. And stopped altogether.

I didn't know if I had killed him, but thought so. I pulled him back and he slumped to the ground. One obstacle removed between me and whatever was happening on Pauline's big boat.

Climbing onto the wall, my wounds screamed at me. I gingerly lowered into that warm and scented water. What was my plan? Well, I wasn't sure, but *crash the party* repeated a few times as I swam.

Nudging the dinghy aside, I struggled up onto the swimming platform at the transom, relieved to see that someone had set the ladder in place. I sloshed upward and over the rail and froze. I had quite the audience.

A dozen or more seemingly delighted and well-dressed wedding guests greeted me with those same dead, oversized eyes I had seen on James Dean. A few had realistic, skin-toned faces. Others were horribly discolored in gray. A few had a dry-leaf color and a papery texture. While they all looked pleased by my arrival, their gazes were looking right through me.

"Hello," I said. No reply expected. No reply received.

I entered the party and walked to the salon door. Inside, the familiar seating area and helm were adorned with white lilies in vases everywhere. Hors d'oeuvres had also been set out on nice silver platters. They were untouched.

I listened for voices and heard none. Entering the short hall beyond, I passed the two familiar berth doors on each side and ignored them. There was a skim of horizontal light along the base of the stateroom door. Music was also beckoning from beyond that fine teak door.

I placed my hand on the door and didn't turn the knob. Instead, I set my ear against the wood.

A male voice was cooing some seriously trite attempts at romantic enticement.

I waited. For Pauline's voice.

The man went on for another minute, and I never heard her say a word.

Holding the 9mm at the ready in one hand, I turned the doorknob with the other.

CHAPTER TWENTY-ONE

◆ ◆ ◆

MUTINY

.

ROLF PULLED on a pair of kneepads and knelt on the deck between Camera Two and the sound tech extending his boom mic down over the shot. The live soundtrack that Deung had insisted upon was causing the sound team real difficulties as they moved the mic in search of a balanced recording. The insipid music entering the set from all directions was wreaking havoc.

"We're close," the tech told Rolf.

"Close?" Rolf grumbled.

The tech tapped his headset and asked for another adjustment from his partner at the soundboard. The two worked together for a minute before the mic tech spoke to Rolf without looking to her.

"We're good."

Rolf didn't reply. Like a few others in the film crew, the reality of what they were about to film was causing a good amount of distaste. Because of the director's growing detachment, Rolf had been breaking the faithful discipline of professional moviemaking and crossing into other's disciplines. Case in point, she was directing, calling the shots, even though she was the assistant producer.

Their director, Rose Daiss, was directly across from her, also kneeling on the other side of the eight-foot opening. She wasn't even looking at the scene, but flipping through the shot log unnecessarily and grimacing.

Rolf looked around to her fellow professionals. They'd worked and reviewed the storyboards countless times. They knew what the scene involved. A few were focused on their craft, but like the director, the lighting tech working both the umbrella and square panel appeared ready to lose his lunch.

Rolf sucked in her lower lip before calling out firmly, "We go in one. Check in."

The sound team called out first. They had it easy, not having to watch, only listen and keep the recording levels primed.

"Cam One—in!"

A plump Asian woman *clacked* the electric shot slate marked up correctly with the Roll, Scene, and Take information. That was good, but the hesitation from the other crew members got Rolf's full attention.

The grip at the extended camera rig was looking down at his shoes instead of his responsibility.

Lighting checked in.

Camera Two right beside her offered a muted, "Cam Two—in…"

The Panavision on the operator's shoulder blocked Rolf's view of her expression.

Rolf looked down into the set.

Pauline Place was being laid on the black velvet bed in her wonderful wedding gown, one nurse gently helping her head back onto a pillow and another nurse reverently adjusting the gown hem so that it resembled a silken bell.

Rolf watched the nurses until they stepped out of view. The actress's expression was limp, and her beautiful eyes were closed. She looked to be at peace and was stunningly lovely. Rolf turned to the dual monitors and saw how Pauline Place was composed in both cameras. Seeing the actress in film instead of in real life heightened the magic that only film composition can provide.

A glance at the director told her she was as disengaged from this shoot as she had been on the wedding set. Rolf again broke protocol and commanded:

"Roll."

She chose to watch the shot on the monitors instead of looking down through the cutaway.

Deung appeared in the frame, entering from the frame bottom, stepping through the stateroom in a cat's stride, roughly in time with the timpani of the soundtrack. He had removed his marriage tuxedo and the snaking scars across his shoulders and his head took on a bloodworm detail in the movie lights.

He approached the foot of the bed. Rolf wanted to turn away, but instead whispered, "So far, so good," to the crew via her headset.

The Spanish bolero swelled and swayed.

Deung's right hand extended and rested on the black velvet, his disfigured fingers pressing deep for balance. He slowly, almost gracefully, climbed up onto the foot of the bed, before his slumbering bride in elegant white.

There was movement among the film crew, a rustling back behind Camera One. Rolf listened to the director climb to her feet.

"Fucking madness. I'm out." Her voice was harsh with disgust.

She departed, but the filming continued.

Two other voices bruised the golden rule of no talking during filming. Rolf tapped her headset and growled to the crew, "We stay in."

The crew, made up of film school dropouts and a couple of ex-studio derelicts, stayed silent.

Deung's hands touched Pauline Place's white silk slippers.

His fingers trembled as he gently pushed on them.

The expanse of the beautiful white gown started to bunch as he guided her slippers upward on the black velvet bed. His hands roamed upward to her shins, riding the gown up, and her knees parted.

Camera One went blank, being set aside.

162 • GREG JOLLEY

The lighting on the composition shifted and dimmed as the tech holding it departed. There was more sickened chatter and movements. Camera Two and sound recording continued.

Rolf turned. These people could work with the dead and worse in any number of current films and here they were, abandoning real life.

She tapped her mic on and cut into all of them.

"You make the disgusting seem normal every day. Stay in!"

There was a short spell of silence. Then the extended boom mic crossed into view of Camera Two—a violation of the worst kind. There was more movement behind Rolf's back.

The filming now had one camera and defused lighting and no sound recording.

On the set, Pauline Place's knees were opening as her shins were pushed further apart.

Pauline opened her eyes.

Rolf turned from the monitor and stared down through the opening. The view was Deung's scarred and discolored back and head above the actress's waist and he had paused, perhaps hearing the ruckus above. It was a slight distraction to what was central in the composition—Pauline Place's face, her eyes, her complicated, bewildered, and frightened expression.

Then the stateroom door swept open.

Rolf was furious, expecting to see a clumsy crew member fall inside.

She tapped her mic to shout, "Cut!"

A fist appeared, tightened around a gun.

CHAPTER TWENTY-TWO

◆ ◆ ◆

DEUNG ESTA MUERTO?

WHEN I opened the stateroom door, I had no idea what to expect, but I was still shocked. On the bed were the heels of fine shoes below a rotund ass in white pants.

Whoever the man was, he was kneeling between the spread legs of a woman in a beautiful white dress. Keeping the 9mm aimed at him, I leaned to my good side and saw who he was with—Pauline.

There were voices and noises from overhead, and I glanced up to a camera and a film crew staring down at me. I shook my head. Figure that out later. Pauline's dazed and hurt expression propelled me.

Movie lingo popped out of my mouth without a thought:

"Hands up, scumbag."

The man raised high enough for me to see hideous injuries deep in the skin of his back. His similarly destroyed face pivoted, and he glared at me and then the gun. I couldn't read his expression clearly because he didn't have much facial muscle to work with.

"Can't," he said in a gargled, lisping voice. "I'll fall."

There was an open glass medical cabinet where normally a nightstand would be beside the bed. The vase of lilies on top did little to add charm. I glanced at the shelves of respirators and drugs and hand-sized medical devices. I looked to Pauline.

"Try," I told him, my finger brushing the trigger.

He appeared to be studying my face, maybe trying to place me. His lidless eyes lowered from the 9mm to my side, the bloody shirt tied around my wound. And that's exactly where his heel struck when he kicked.

The pain was stunning. I never knew pain could get that vicious, that radiant. The gun hit the floor as I did. I groaned. I bellowed. He was over me and kicking, landing strikes to my ribs and my head over and over. I curled up, trying to protect myself from blow after blow.

The hideous monster had me. My head bounced off the floor from a solid kick. I believed my life was ending. His shoe smashed into my lower back and my legs arched in reaction, my feet tangled with his, tripping his balance. He fell.

I heard screams and calls from above the bed. The blows stopped. I'd like to say I searched for the 9mm, but I didn't. I couldn't. I rolled onto my back and looked at him.

He was getting back to his feet. I watched him rise. I stole a look at Pauline. He stepped over beside me and cocked his shoe and I saw that my head was the target.

He kicked, and the side of my head took it full force. Thinking froze. All light and sound died.

◆ ◆ ◆

I CAME to, still in the stateroom, lying on the floor, staring at a table leg. A veined, ruined hand holding my 9mm came into view.

I heard shouting and yelling from a hundred miles away and from all directions.

My muscles screamed as I rolled over to the door. Perhaps it was instinct to escape. Don't know.

A moment passed. Ten seconds? Twenty seconds? Don't know. The gun didn't fire.

A strong voice rose among the shrill ones. A deep and firm command.

"Enough!"

Between me and the door another pair of shiny black shoes appeared. I expected those shoes to take up where the other pair had left off. I rotated my head, painfully, and looked.

I distantly recognized the silver-haired man from the filming pool. He was soaking wet from the waist on up.

My thinking was clearing some. If thoughts are like film, mine were flickering.

The man I had tried to drown was speaking.

"…was with you with your collecting and playing with the dead. But not this."

There was a struggle above me. Grunts and curses.

A gun fired. I didn't feel an impact. I saw the silver-haired man arch back as a bullet struck him in the chest.

The gun fired three more times.

The silver-haired man above me extend a long, silver gun. It was an entirely different creature. When he pulled the trigger, the weapon roared.

That same gun hit the floor. The man's knees buckled, and he crumbled between me and the door. He landed and didn't move.

I stared. My mind cleared a little more. Enough to panic about the other guy behind me. I rolled over. The pain was terrible, but not as bad as before. When I turned fully around, I saw the other man. The back of his ugly head had splattered the bed. He wasn't moving. His eyes were open wide with surprise.

New voices entered the stateroom. A pair of legs stepped over me. My 9mm was kicked and slid away. Whatever had been in the silver-haired man's gun had apparently discharged more than one bullet. His target had three bloody chest wounds. He lay at the base of the bed.

The bed.

People were shouting and moving about the room. I heard Pauline's name being repeated. I listened for her voice as I stared at that shirtless monster. Even with the weaving scars and burn tissue and errant and dark suture scars, the bullet holes were clear. They were dark, deep, torn holes, blood red.

There was a dime-sized round hole in his chest. I looked into his lidless eyes. A blood-filled hole was punched in between them, destroying the bridge of his nose.

A gruff-looking man knelt before me. The borrowed director's lens hanging from his neck nearly clouted me in the face. His hands gently gripped my shoulders.

"Bro, you are seriously injured, but you're gonna get help, okay?"

"Help me sit up."

I wanted a better view of that black bed.

He helped me up and continued talking. Other voices as well, most yelling and shouting. I leaned back against the wall across from the bed.

"How is she?" I asked. No one answered. My voice was weak and bubbly. More people racing into the stateroom.

I couldn't see much of Pauline with so many attending her. Two nurses and film crew members were swarming the bed. I caught glimpses of her white gown.

A fight broke out in the sort hall. Scuffling and arguing and shouting in Spanish and English. I looked in that direction, past the silver-haired man's body. A man in a wet security uniform was struggling to get into the room. A couple of strong men—film crew members—aggressively forcing him back.

"Fuck off, Tacas," the taller of the two said. "Your boss is a stiff."

The guard looked around him and at the dead man with the bullet hole in the center of his face.

"*Deung esta muerto?*"

So now I knew the monster's name. Not that it meant anything to me.

"*Deung y Allister estan muertos!*" the guard shouted back into the hall.

The fighting stopped and the shouting fell to a hush.

Activity continued around the black bed.

"How is she?" I repeated, my voice stronger.

No one answered. A hand extended back toward me in a stop gesture.

A man in a business suit squeezed into the room. He picked up the 9mm and that long, mean handgun beside the silver-haired man. Stepping past me, he carried both from the room, holding them by their trigger guards.

I followed him with my gaze as he pressed his way through the clog of people in the doorway.

I looked up. Inside the square hole cut in the ceiling, a shoulder-mount camera was still running—I saw the red light to the left of the lens. The woman beside it was looking down into the chaos. She was smiling and mouthing into her headset mic.

"Turn it off!" I screamed at her.

She didn't.

I lowered my eyes to the activities around that black bed.

I know my mind wasn't clear. Not yet connecting all the dots. That said, I took the deepest breath possible and roared.

"Is—she—okay?"

CHAPTER TWENTY-THREE

◆ ◆ ◆

SOLDIERS AND POLICE

I INSISTED on remaining aboard the mock *Viewfinder* until Pauline was assisted onto dry land. My new friend, Justin—he of the dangling director's lens—helped me to my feet and through the boat and out on the deck. It was crowded, and no one was moving.

"Care to sit?" he asked, and I nodded.

We eased through the wedding party to the port bench. I took the narrow space beside a very dead and dried woman in a festive cocktail dress.

"Join me?" I asked Justin.

"There's no room. She's in my way."

At that, one of the security guards who had followed us from the stateroom stepped in, hefted the woman, and threw her over the rail.

The water splashed.

The guard grinned.

I stared.

Justin sat down. "*Gracias.*"

I heard laughter. What the guard had done was inspiring his compadres.

During the next two minutes the stern deck was almost cleared and roomy, and the pool around the fake boat was littered with bodies. Tacas—Deung's former employee—came out on deck. He saw what was going on and when a hesitant, cowering member of the house staff raised his hands and shook his head, Tacas said, "Let 'em. We'll fish 'em out later and bury them."

More of the dead were tipped and tossed over the rails. Within a minute, the deck was cleared. Those doing the pushing enjoyed themselves, growing boisterous, and when there were no more partygoers to push, they went down the ramp as a crowd and headed off.

"May I join you?" Tacas asked.

I nodded, and he sat down on Justin's side.

We listened to the voices carrying off into other parts of the building. I looked to Justin, who was staring straight up at the night sky and stars painted on the ceiling.

"It's almost over," Tacas said. His voice was reluctant and resolved.

I was forming a reply, not sure what I was going to say. It turned out I didn't need to. House staff directed by the two nurses carefully and slowly carried Pauline out on a stretcher.

I stood. She was being surrounded and tenderly cared for. I couldn't see her face, but could tell that she was in gentle hands. They carried her across the plank and down the ramp.

"I radioed Deung's copter with instructions," Tacas said. "She'll be in hospital in thirty-five minutes."

I continued watching the group helping Pauline.

"Thank you," I said, not turning.

Justin stood and took my arm. "Come on, bro, let's get you some care."

I nodded, seeing the tail end of Pauline's group disappear into the shadows of the soundstage.

Justin and I crossed the stern deck. Before we left the boat, I heard Tacas speak to his radiophone. It was a brief, contentious exchange.

We started across to the ramp, over the water where two cadavers were sinking.

"They're raiding the residence. They'll find a few diamond trays," Tacas said. "They'll celebrate and fill their pockets. And they should. I've got my own pocketful."

I paused and considered what to say. Justin nudged my shoulder with his hand, and we left without replying. He and I crossed over onto dry land and turned in the direction Pauline had been carried off.

◆ ◆ ◆

ENTERING DEUNG'S residence, I was struck by the contrast to Pauline's villa. While her temporary residence with Sara was a study of unwelcoming darkness up front, and all the life and light protected within, Deung's cavernous and still entrance was but a barren shell behind a grand façade. Justin and I turned and went back outside into the cool shade of the grand portico. We walked slowly between the center columns, where I asked to sit down.

Justin helped me down on the top marble step. Someone handed me a damp towel that I will forever be grateful for. I wiped my face with its wet fabric and sucked moisture into my mouth.

Out beyond the wide stairs, the manicured lawn reached out for two-hundred yards in all directions until it abutted the dense jungle. The sky was a peerless blue, and off to our left, a black helicopter was warming up, with the nurses standing at the cargo door, watching until it slid closed.

The engine revved, and thirty seconds later the rotors were spinning.

The nurses turned and ran toward the residence as the helicopter rose. The copter looked steady and sure. After elevating fifty yards, its nose tipped, and the craft flew off, rising steadily and looking to easily clear the jungle roof. I watched until the copter with my ex-wife inside flew out of view to the north.

A silence filled the void in the impressive view.

Justin squeezed my shoulder. "Should be back in a few," he told me. "Got something to take care of."

"Sure," I replied. I just wanted to sit there with my damp rag, looking at the quiet grounds down below.

"I'll also get you some help," he added.

◆ ◆ ◆

WITHIN THE next ninety minutes, three large helicopters landed out on the lawn. Each was much larger than Deung's; one belonged to the police, and the other two were military. Soldiers and police debarked first, with civilians following them at a more cautious pace. The soldiers led the police contingency across the lawn and up the wide stairs washed in heat and sunlight. They moved past me on both sides and entered the building. One soldier returned two minutes later and squatted before me on the steps. His uniform had a medical emblem on the chest. He set a pack down and opened it.

I answered his questions as best I could. I was given three shots and a respirator and told to lay back. He was calm and professional and carefully opened the bloody shirt wrapped around my wounds.

At least one of those shots was anesthetic, as I was soon hovering a bit and feeling little pain; in fact, I was distantly following the movements of his hands and instruments on the middle of my body while I stared upward. Far above, the portico ceiling was ornate with design. While the medic did what I am sure was his professional best, I tried for a bit to make sense of the fanciful designs. I heard Justin return and sit down beside me. He said to the medic or me, "They started a fire."

I had no thoughts about that one way or another.

There was a sharp pain and I called out. I was given another injection and was soon floating halfway to the portico ceiling.

Sometime later, I was transferred over into a stretcher and lifted and carried down the stairs. Halfway down, I could smell the grass and helicopter fumes. After I was secured inside the cargo bay, additional medical treatment began. I watched a second medic assist the first, noting that Justin was seated at my side with a black backpack.

"This is for you," he told me, indicating the pack.

His hand took ahold of mine and over the next hour and a half, he never let up. I drifted in and out, thanking the stars above for the miracle of modern medication.

Our copter was the first to depart, all seats taken and the cargo area around me laden with trunks and suitcases. Two soldiers with automatic weapons sat with Justin and me and the medics. Their focus was on the suitcases. Justin let go of my hand to squeeze into a jump seat and belt in, as did the others. My stretcher had already been secured.

Unlike the copter carrying Pauline away to safety and care, ours rose fast and aggressively pivoted before roaring off with its nose down. Someone placed a headset on me, and my ears were filled with flight commands and rapid conversations in Spanish. During the first pause in the loud chatter, Justin spoke up.

"There goes the compound. I see three—no, four fires."

CHAPTER TWENTY-FOUR

♦ ♦ ♦

TELEGRAM

IN THE States, hospitals look more like Hilton hotels and function much the same. The hospital in Puerto Mita was a four-story building that resembled a birthday cake more than anything. It was set back from the main cobblestone thoroughfare with a courtyard entrance alive with color from flowers in full bloom.

My three days there were spent in a room at the end of the hall on the second floor. All of the medical equipment was modern, and the doctors and nurses were professional and kind.

Pauline's room was up on the fourth floor. I was told it was more of a suite and had a view of the ocean over the local rooftops.

I was glad to be set aside, so to speak, as I heard that the fourth floor was a circus, as was the courtyard and entrance. My doctor described the media and authorities and studio representatives as *tenso*, which I interpreted as *all wound up*.

I would have been released sooner, but an infection in the exit wound kept me there. I learned that I had no organ damage, just a hole through my muscle and fat. I'm sure I was also kept to be questioned, which was a bit intense those first two days.

When Sara came by in the morning of the second day and told me that Pauline was fine and all of the nasty drugs had been flushed from her body, I was relieved and pleased.

"The plan is to whisk her out the back of the hospital during the 1:00 p.m. media status."

"She still doing well?" I asked.

"Yes. And she's very grateful. She's weak and a little confused, but getting well fast."

"You watch over her. Take good care of her. As always."

"Yes. As best I can."

"Your best is very good."

Sara's cellphone was going nuts, call after call and texts. Discordant notes of different music and sounds.

"Go," I said. "Care for her. I'll come by when I can."

"The villa?" she asked, looking out my window to the lovely view of a rooftop AC unit. "Umm."

She gave me a kiss and left, taking a call.

When I left the hospital the next day, the only sign of the media event was in the lovely, welcoming courtyard. Most of the beautiful flowers were trampled. All I was carrying was the backpack Justin had given me and a Ziploc bag with my personal belongings and medicine bottles.

Standing in sunlight for the first time in days, I had to grin. The Willy was parked in the shade of a massive tree.

"We've kept a watch on it," the parking attendant explained and handed me the keys.

"Thank you," I replied and gave him two twenties from my wallet in the Ziploc. After crossing to the old Jeep and gazing in, I returned to the attendant and gave him a hundred.

The Willy started after a small fit of hesitation and coughing. I pulled my old satchel off the passenger floorboard and set it beside the backpack. Putting the Ziploc inside, I was pleased to see my few odd belongings. I considered putting the backpack contents into the satchel as well, but I suspected I wouldn't have them long.

Before I put the Willy in gear, I climbed out and set the windshield flat over the hood. I knew I'd be eating bugs and for once was okay with that. I wanted fresh streaming air. I drove away with a smile to the wind.

Took me twenty minutes to get to a beach with nearby parking. To the north past the harbor was a scenic stretch of beach and waves, complete with colorful cabanas and tourists and vendors. Everyone looked happy and content. It was a fine, sunny day.

I shouldered my satchel and carried the backpack in my hand as I walked to the south. A stone-lined culvert extended from a seaside restaurant to the surf. The water washing along in it was smooth and clear.

Ignoring the pleasant voices and music from the restaurant veranda, I set my satchel in the sand and walked along the water flowing along the curve of stones and into the sea, to shin depth. After dropping the backpack, I opened it, letting corrosive salt water in.

I thanked my new dear friend Justin again as I took out each of the three compact data drives of footage. I crushed each with a hand-sized rock. When the three electronic boxes were mashed and a mess of exposed insides, I let them soak in saltwater.

I was tempted to fling each into the waves but decided not to litter. I let the corrosive magic of saltwater work for twenty minutes. Beside the culvert, delighted children and adults and vendors were having a good time on their holidays.

I scooped up the three ruined data drives, carried them up the beach, and dropped one in each of the three trash cans I passed along the boardwalk back to the Willy. I gave the empty backpack to the first child I saw—a girl sitting on a stool beside a cart of dirty dishes at the rear door of a cantina.

◆ ◆ ◆

IT TOOK longer than I care to admit to find my way to Pauline's villa. I drove up the drive and parked to the side in the first open space, a hundred yards from the residence. As before, the villa was dark and overgrown and uninviting. That didn't matter; the media and what I assumed were government vehicles had welcomed themselves. A group of reporters and officials were milling about the base of the steps to the closed doors.

Their vibe was bored and barely patient. Security guards stood to both sides of the big front door, and I saw that I wasn't going to get side yard access—those approaches were also guarded. The press and officials looked to be in pre-fiesta mode. I knew they and the cameras would all light up whenever that front door opened.

I stood just back from the small crowd, in between a television van and a nondescript sedan. I double-checked the satchel and wished I had a phone. When a hand gripped my elbow, I turned and there was Sara in a battered sun hat and dark glasses.

"We've been watching from the window." She smiled. "The Willy was spotted. Come."

Sara's stride was like a magic wand. We were allowed onto the walk alongside the dark mansion, stepping through creeping overgrowth on the stone path to the other side of the villa. The two guards at the back of the residence nodded to her, but she had to speak to each briefly before I was allowed access. She and I crossed the pool deck and stepped inside the chilled air of Pauline's brightly lit and comfortable living area.

Sara hooked her sunglasses into the top of her dress and tossed the beach hat.

"Something to drink? Eat?" she asked.

I studied her face, which was still bruised from Ethan's attack some days before.

"You're okay? Water, please, if you're having one."

She went to the kitchen and got a bottle from the refrigerator. I noted that there were no house staff present.

Sara twisted the cap off the bottle for me and I took a drink, looking into the large room. Right away I saw the empty bookcases. There was an open travel crate beside Sara's desk.

"She's gone," I said.

"Yes, Pierce. We got her out, yesterday. So far, no one knows."

"Just let the circus out front figure it out on their own."

"Yep. As always, they'll spin themselves silly and move on to the next spectacle."

"That's their job."

We shared a smile.

"Pauline is very grateful for all you did for her."

I didn't reply, but it was nice to hear.

"Sit, please," Sara offered.

I looked about the living space.

"I don't think I'll be sticking around long."

She circled to the long, low table before the couch where her pillow and blankets lay. Taking up an envelope, she brought it over to me.

"She left this for you," she said.

Instead of opening the envelop, I pocketed it.

"You take good care of her, okay?" I said and softly kissed her cheek.

"Of course. I'm leaving this evening. After dark."

"Our boys?" I asked.

"Bill and Tim are still being watched, but not intruded on. They're fine and safe and completely in the dark about all of this."

That brought a smile and I enjoyed it.

"I don't know what's in the envelope," Sara said, "so I might be repeating—but that insane divorce agreement has been both trashed and killed."

"We're still married?"

"Believe so, yes. And you're welcome to stay here as long as you like. Rest up and heal."

"Darling Sara. Thank you. I think I'll head out. Do I need permission to leave?" I asked, looking to the poolside security guard.

"You know better," Sara kidded, and she was right.

Entering these movie star *situations* was impossible, but leaving them was as simple as keeping your eyes to your shoes and your lips zipped until you reached your vehicle and drove away. After giving Sara a hug, that's exactly what I did. A few minutes later, I was out on another narrow jungle road. The breezing air was welcomed, and I was confident that I'd be lost again in a few miles.

◆ ◆ ◆

I PARKED the Willy between a dumpster and the rear of a cargo truck and sat in the heat, swatting insects and listening to my old Jeep's fine but tired engine click and ping. After finishing the last of the water bottle Sara had given me, I opened the envelope.

Inside was a telegram. Just seeing it brightened my spirits—it was one of the many good and eccentric ways of the wonderful Pauline Place.

The first lines confirmed what Sara had already told me. Our sons were safe, and the security was watching over them and being tactfully nonintrusive in their good and normal lives.

The next line wasn't a surprise. It was why I had parked the Willy here.

THE VIEWFINDER IS NOW YOURS -(STOP)-
MAY I NEVER SEE IT OR THINK OF IT AGAIN
EXCEPT AS A REMINDER OF OUR SIMPLER DAYS
-(STOP)- I'VE ARRANGED FOR THE WILLY TO BE
TRANSPORTED TO THE STATES -(STOP)-

A lengthy paragraph followed. It began, "My darling Pierce," and no, you don't get to know what she wrote.

I stashed the telegram inside my satchel, gathered it up, and climbed out.

The street boy who had previously watched over the Willy was right there again, watching me expectantly.

"*Señor, las llaves por favor,*" the boy, little more than a child, instructed me.

I handed him the keys. He pocketed them and climbed in on the rear jump seat and turned so he could, I assume, watch for anyone who might approach. I noted the elderly woman in the doorway who had his back.

Before I left, I took out five twenties and pressed them into his hand.

"*Gracias*," I said and walked back up along the road that paralleled the docks and rows of dispirited fishing craft.

At the end of the center dock, I sat down on the filthy, crusty boards and took off my left shoe. I was unlacing the right one, but stopped, realizing that I wouldn't have to swim.

Walton was gliding the dinghy from the *Viewfinder* across the still and suspect water of the harbor channel. When the dinghy bumped against the boards, I climbed in, holding my satchel and left shoe.

Walton looked resplendent. She was in spotless shorts and a T-shirt and looked pleased, offering me a sideways pirate's smile. I sat in the bow. While she took us across, I watched her work-smudged hands steer the dinghy. As always, she was looking focused and curious at the same time.

When we were up aboard the *Viewfinder*, it was a bit disconcerting; I'd been on that mock version just days ago, complete with cameras and lights and equipment. And nicely dressed-up dead people. The immaculate wooden deck was welcomed.

Walton headed inside the salon and I stayed right there, looking up at the flying bridge where I assumed she still lived.

"So now you're the owner," she called. "That works. Been talking with Sara. A few things, but first, where shall I chart for?"

"Can the boat make it to Detroit?"

"Are you being funny?"

"I don't think so."

"Off the top of my head, yes. The boat itself is fine. I need an hour with the charts. Wouldn't be a quick trip."

"I'm not in a hurry. You?"

"I'm in a hurry to leave this nasty harbor and sleep inside instead of up there. Other than that, I've got all the time in the world."

All the time in the world. I liked that. I believed I had the same.

I sat down on the rail bench in the same spot I had shared with Justin when the celebrations and fires had begun on Deung's estate. I took off my other shoe.

It was nice to be barefoot. To be on a clean and normal boat. To be with a good and capable friend who was already cooking up a plan and route to get me home.

Walton peeked out through the door and looked me over without a word. I had removed my shirt and was enjoying the sun on my skin.

"Change into a swimsuit," she said. "Sara sent over a couple of suitcases and a briefcase. Get comfortable. I'll be a while."

"Thank you, I'm fine," I replied.

And I was. For a bit. When the heat and humidity had worked me over, I went inside and opened one of the suitcases. I took a pair of swim trunks into the hall bath, where I stripped and pulled it on while standing in a cool shower.

"Better?" Walton asked.

She was leaning over charts and opened reference books on the galley table. Her eyes didn't rise, but a lovely smile shone.

"Better, yes," I answered and sat at the table to watch her.

She was working the main chart with both a protractor triangle and a parallel ruler.

"Short answer," she said, watching her own fingers just above a pencil tip. "It's doable. There are actually two courses once we get to the Atlantic. My short estimate is fifty-six days."

"At a leisurely pace?"

"You know, I actually padded for that. You okay with leaving at first light? I'd like to get south to Puerto de Manzanillo to do the supply and fuel. Sure as sin not gonna do it here."

"You're the captain."

"Why yes, I am." Her smile widened. She kept her eyes on her work.

I watched until she looked up and across the galley.

"Trip like this is going to be costly. I'll plot our stops, but Pierce?"

"Yes?"

"You funded for this?"

Walton was looking at a Packard restoration mechanic, not the boat owner or the husband of a movie star.

"It's funny…" I started. Instead of answering her, I got up and went to the two suitcases. "It's a Danser family *thing*," I said, likely muddying the waters all the more.

I lifted the old Samsonite briefcase from between the suitcases and brought it back to the table.

I didn't open it. Didn't need to.

"We're good," I told her and set the briefcase at my side.

◆ ◆ ◆

FOR A number of days, the Mexican coast was within sight with binoculars up on the flying bridge. During the first five days, I often thought of my brother, Jared, who had been alongside Pauline and me on a boating adventure many years before. Easier, simpler, and often stranger times—long ago, but easy to recall.

Walton operated the boat and I helped any way I could. For starters, I took on the cooking and house-cleaning responsibilities. Walton preferred the flying bridge to the helm inside, and when I climbed to sit with her, she was often into her well-worn books about recovery. I found these interesting and read portions of a few, but I had climbed more for conversation, which was not readily available.

On the first day out, we negotiated our sleeping arrangements. She initially insisted that I take the forward stateroom, but that simply wasn't going to happen. There were too many distant and recent memories of that space: the recent filmmaking in a mock-up version the strongest. She took the room, and I bunked in the starboard-side berth in the hall.

She taught me the radios. After a couple of days, I could navigate the dials and displays and observe the rules and procedures. Soon I was talking with family and friends on the landside world. The days slowed, and yakking on the radios filled many hours. I checked on Pauline daily by calling and annoying Sara. I talked to my sons on alternating days and enjoyed an occasional fun and very random conversation with my good friend, Ryan Dot. I also spent at least an hour or two on the line with Rhonda, who was at first perplexed and then delighted and amused by my questions and slowly evolving plans.

We passed through the Panama Canal, Walton expertly captaining the *Viewfinder* through the elevating locks while I did my best to assist during the maneuvers.

She or I opened the briefcase nine times during our sea journey, which took seventy-three days.

We ate dinner together in the galley most nights and it was during our meals together that our relationship turned from fluid and jelled. When I joined her up on the flying bridge during the day, she was often reading and at the same time having lively and funny conversations with other boats and ships and harbor authorities. When we sat at the galley table in the evening, she and I talked about our good, odd friends. It came to me that she and I were like two radios with a common frequency. We heard each other clearly.

◆ ◆ ◆

WE MOORED the *Viewfinder* in the waters just out beyond the Detroit Yacht Club on the private island adjacent to Belle Isle. Walton negotiated a slip, and three days later she and I stepped down onto solid and steady ground.

We parted ways, with Walton staying behind to work an impressively detailed list of maintenance tasks. I offered to stay on and help, and she shooed me off. She was focused on having the boat fully serviced and then winterized. We made plans for a dinner with

Dot the following week. She had grown increasingly interested in him and his work at Howie's Restoration.

I rented a car, specifically asking for "A Buick. Any model, but a new one."

I got a current-year Regal. Sapphire blue metallic with an ebony leather interior. I headed out driving on pavement, which was a novelty for the first twenty miles. Then freeways. And traffic and so long, novelty.

When I arrived home, I sat at my kitchen table and took inventory.

My sons were fine.

Pauline was fine. She and Sara were preparing for the rescheduled completion of the movie *Black Island*, here in the States.

My house was fine. My weekly housekeeper had continued even though I hadn't paid her forward. The pantry was restocked, and the refrigerator freshly filled. The stack of mail, mostly bills, was a pleasant distraction. I went out on the back deck and looked at the lake. It was as close as I wanted to be to water for a while.

It was good to sleep in my bed, or any bed that didn't sway. In the morning, I ate a bowl of cereal, dialed Gustin's, and resigned as gratefully as possible. My next call was to Rhonda.

CHAPTER TWENTY-FIVE

◆ ◆ ◆

SEVEN MONTHS LATER

EXIT 56 is a few miles north of Ann Arbor and it doesn't have a name, like so many turnoffs along Highway 23. If you turn right at the stop sign, there's a gas station with a minimarket; beyond, the narrow two-lane becomes a dirt road before entering the trees toward Wildwood Lake. Turning to the left, you go over the bridge and the westbound crumbling road that runs straight through tall green trees and wild grass. For many years there had been a roadside diner located at the base of the bridge, to the left. It had been abandoned and shuttered for many years. Traffic was sparse as the road served few residences some miles away in both directions.

With Rhonda's invaluable, persuasive negotiation skills, she and I had maneuvered the local and state government and corporate tangle of paths, aided by hefty *pulls* from the briefcase. It helped that the scale of our plan had been small, entering a geographical market that, as one corporate representative said to a government representative during one of our meetings, was *ridiculous*. Once Rhonda and I had the ball rolling with these folks, I turned to the site itself and the new construction. The building was a small affair, minute by industry standards, and was built quickly, using all the latest technologies and materials.

On opening day, I had three Jeeps in the showroom. There was enough space on the fine reflective floor for maybe two more of the new Willys, in what the corporation knew as the smallest Jeep dealership in the States. And the free world.

The showroom gleamed, a celebration of the latest technologies. There were large, interactive displays of the new model's features. The air conditioning was scented and fresh and carried the melodies of only the very latest in music.

Before I stepped inside for my first day on the sales floor, I looked up at the electronic sign atop the shimmering glass and metal dealership. The sign read, simply, "Modern Willys."

One of the many battles Rhonda and I had fought and won was for permission to open a Jeep dealership that only sold one model. The three Willys under the track lighting glimmered and showed off their contemporary design and features. The three were identical save their paint; one sandy, one blue, and one white.

Sitting down on the new leather couch before a coffee table, I looked out the storefront windows. After fifteen minutes, I actually saw a potential customer pass by; a pickup truck loaded with what looked like irrigation equipment.

My cellphone purred. I took it out of my pocket and looked across the showroom, feeling pleased with what Rhonda and I and the briefcase had accomplished in a very short time.

"We're running a bit late," Walton said.

I heard my good friend Ryan Dot mouthing off and then laughing from her side, behind the wheel.

"A few minutes late should be fine," I said.

The parking lot out front was as barren of customers as the showroom.

Rhonda had suggested I send up stringers of helium balloons. It was a great idea, and I had forgotten. I'm sure they would have had a significant positive effect on the turnout, such as it already was. A

familiar squirrel crossed the lot in unhurried stride. A week ago, I'd
watched its hesitant movements. I believe it now felt it safe to cross at
leisure. It scampered off across the freshly mowed lawn and bounded
out of view to my right.

A glint of sun on chrome caught my attention. I watched Dot and
Walton crest the bridge and start toward me. Dot was driving slowly as
was his way, guiding his '53 Buick Roadmaster at its 1950's pace.

I went outside as they pulled in, waving to Walton and circling
the old vehicle to Dot's window. He rolled it down. There was my
very good friend, smiling at me and the dealership.

"Glad you could make it," I greeted him. "Do me a favor? Park
this old thing in back."

Dot squeezed my hand on the windowsill, put the Roadmaster
in gear, and drove off around to the rear of Modern Willys.

We met up in the showroom and sat across from each other
on the couches. There were none of the old-school sales desks and
chairs in the place.

"Congratulations," Dot offered sincerely, and I thanked him while
Walton took up a customer iPad from the table and began to explore.

"Howie sends his best," Dot added. Because I asked, he brought
me up to speed on the recent Packard restoration efforts that he was
working. With the economy chugging along and no longer belly to
the sky, Howie's was a busy place. Many new collectors were getting
into the game.

My new hire, Trent, was crossing the floor to us. Trent was
fresh from the University of Michigan with a dual major in the
latest automobile technology and marketing. He had an office and
I didn't. He spent most of his time on his three computers, large
monitors, and tablets. I had no idea what he was doing. Trent was
pleasant and smart and nice to have around. He was carrying a
Willy-logoed canvas cooler, which he placed before us on the table.
He set out four glasses, filled them with ice cubes, and placed four
bottles of Fanta Grape before us.

"Cheers." He grinned to the Dot and Walton. "And thank you for coming to the grand opening."

Dot opened a bottle for Walton and poured for her. She was busy, her lovely, intelligent eyes scanning as her fingertips scrolled images and traced lines of information on the iPad.

I poured for Trent and offered him the seat beside me. He eased past to sit, but didn't.

"I think we have a customer," he said, looking to the windows.

A shiny, new, black town car was turning off the narrow road and gliding into the parking lot. The long, black car rolled slowly to a stop just back from the main doors.

"If this is the customer that emailed, she'll want to take the white one for a spin," I said to Trent. "Please back it out."

Trent went off to unlock and open the double glass doors at the other side of the showroom.

The driver climbed out and looked across through the dealership windows. He wore a black suit, white shirt, and was a big, strong man. After looking us over, he offered a pleasant smile.

I crossed to the glass door as it whirred upward for Trent to get the Willy out. The driver walked to the rear of the limo and stopped. I expected him to round to one of the passenger doors. He used a fob to pop the trunk as Trent steered the white Willy around to the front of the lot and parked.

The tinted rear door window of the long car lowered.

Dot's delightful laughter followed me as I walked out to the town car.

The driver carried a small suitcase over to the Willy and placed it in the back seat.

I stepped before the lowered window and gazed in, my thoughts and heart in a swirl. Pauline and I spoke a few words, but I believe the real conversation was between our eyes.

I heard the door unlock. Before I opened the door for her, I turned and called to Dot.

"Says she wants to take a test drive."

ABOUT THE AUTHOR

Greg Jolley earned a Master of Arts in Writing from the University of San Francisco and lives in the very small town of Ormond Beach, Florida. When not writing, he is a student and researcher of historical crime, primarily those of the 1800s.